According to St. John

A DETECTIVE NOVEL

by William Babula

A Lyle Stuart / Irma Heldman Book
Published by Carol Communications

Copyright © 1989 by William Babula

A Lyle Stuart Book
Published by Carol Communications

Editorial Offices
600 Madison Avenue
New York, NY 10022

Sales & Distribution Offices
120 Enterprise Avenue
Secaucus, NJ 07094

In Canada: Musson Book Company
A division of General Publishing Co. Limited
Don Mills, Ontario

All rights reserved. No part of this book
may be reproduced in any form, except by
a newspaper or magazine reviewer who wishes
to quote brief passages in connection
with a review.

Queries regarding rights and permissions
should be addressed to: Carol Communications,
600 Madison Avenue, New York, NY 10022

Manufactured in the United States of America

Library of Congress Cataloging-in-Publication Data

Babula, William.
   According to St. John / by William Babula.
      p.   cm.
   "A Lyle Stuart / Irma Heldman Book"
   I. Title. II. Title: According to Saint John.
PS3552.A252A65   1989
813'.54--dc 19   88-37562
                                                                        CIP

For KAREN, JARED, and JOELLE
The Family

According to
to
St. John

1

It was a typical Monday morning at the St. John Detective Agency. I was at my desk in the office and my two partners were late.

I got out the file for the brokerage house fraud case I was working on and started going through it again. I had to come up with a strategy I could sell to management. So far it hadn't been easy.

I was on the edge of a good idea when the outer door opened. I heard the click of high heels. One partner, Michelle "Mickey" Farabaugh, had arrived. She moved around in her office for a minute. When she came into mine—the third one back from the entrance—wearing a tight cashmere sweater and short wool skirt the good idea I was so close to slipped away.

After we exchanged good mornings I tried to retrieve it. And failed. So I settled for leaning back and admiring Mickey's five-foot-eight classic hourglass of a figure. With a subtlety appropriate to a private investigator.

This partner had joined my San Francisco agency a little over a year ago after some time at Ohio State and some time on an Ohio city police force. It was going to be her career until she got booted off the force for appearing—one photo only—in a *Playboy* "Women in Blue" pictorial.

Mickey told me about it when I interviewed her for the job. She admitted it was unprofessional, certainly unliberated, then flashed a mischievous grin and said, "Every woman should pose nude at least once in her life."

If she looked like Mickey Farabaugh I thought. But I didn't say a word.

I just hired her and spent the rest of the day tracking down a back issue of the magazine. It was basic detective work. If you can't do a little job like that you shouldn't be in the gumshoe business.

The title was misleading; she wasn't dressed in blue or anything else in the quarter-page glossy photo. All she was wearing was a smile and a rocking chair. Policeperson at leisure.

Mickey moved across the room and put her hands on the back of a chair in front of my desk. She tossed back her shoulder-length honey blond hair and showed a crescent of perfect teeth. Those green eyes glowed. Something had to be up.

"I got a call from my old roommate at Ohio State over the weekend. Denny Belknap."

"Oh? That's nice. What's he doing these days?" A P.I. must always keep cool. So I did.

Mickey and I had a brief romance which she doused with the emotional equivalent of ice water. She decided that a personal relationship in such a small office was a hell of a distraction. She wanted a purely professional arrangement in the St. John Detective Agency despite all of the brilliant arguments to the contrary by me, the eponymous founder of said agency.

She smiled again.

"Denny is short for Denise, my *female* roommate's name, Jeremiah. You're always jumping to conclusions."

"Sometimes that's the only way to solve a case." She'd set me up. That was okay with me. Maybe all was not lost between us.

"Denny's an actress. She has a part in the new *Macbeth* that Perry Maydik is directing at the Marina Theater."

Perry Maydik was a rising star among directors. A black man, as

According to St. John

a Shakespearean actor he had moved from a type-cast Othello to parts conventionally played by whites, including Hamlet and even a rather youthful Lear. As a Shakespearean director he was equally innovative.

In my undergraduate days at Berkeley and elsewhere I studied drama and acting. I thought that would be the best preparation for what had been my ultimate goal: law school.

"Good for your old roommate. Maydik's a major talent."

"Amanda Cole's Lady Macbeth."

"She should add something."

Amanda Cole was a legendary star with a reputation for being temperamental. Recently her career had taken a downward turn and she had been reduced to bit parts in B movies. But at least they had kept her in front of the public.

"There will be three comps at the box office for us courtesy of Denny Belknap for the gala opening and post-performance reception tomorrow night."

"Just like in the P.I. business, it pays to know the right people."

"I knew you'd be pleased but do you think the Chief will want to go?"

"Of course. But only after we go through the usual stalling routine. 'White man's bullshit culture, etc.' " I did a pretty good imitation of the Chief. Especially when he wasn't around to critique it.

"I don't know."

The front door opened and I heard the heavy footsteps of my other partner, Chief Moses Tamiami, a formidable Florida Seminole, as he came in. A few moments later he strode into my office, glowering.

The ever-observant Mickey asked, "What's bothering you, Chief?"

"This is October 12. Columbus Day."

The Chief pointed to the black armband he wore around a monstrous left bicep.

I rolled my eyes at Mickey. We went through this a year ago.

The Chief shook his mane of black hair and looked down his classic Indian nose at me from his six feet seven inches. His height and a muscular frame that easily carried three hundred pounds made him a lot more than plain imposing. It was like having a black bear rear up on its hind legs in front of me. Only this creature was wearing a Florida State Seminole football jersey, complete with a Seminole head on the front that resembled the Chief himself and the number one on the back. The jerseys were a reminder of his brief stint in the offensive line at FSU. He now ordered them by the dozen with different numbers for his ladies. He called them party favors.

"About this white man Christopher Columbus. He is the original illegal alien. You give one of them amnesty and look what happens." He made a sweeping gesture that took in North, South, and Central America.

"Chief. Come on. I've got us a perk." Mickey said.

The Chief sat down on the worn leather couch against the far wall by the coat rack and a palm in a ceramic pot. "And I have got the blues."

"Shouldn't happen to a red man," I said.

He just looked at me and squinted. If looks could scalp. . .

Mickey told him about Denny and the play and the party.

Chief Moses stretched out. "Does this mean we must go?"

Mickey and the Chief. My crack investigation team. Mickey was high-tech; Chief Moses was like a raw force of nature. Like the wind or the sea. When he wanted to be.

We were into a ritual.

The Chief got up and stepped behind my desk. He looked at the tangle of vegetation in my urban backyard. He didn't approve of how I treated the land.

"Shakespeare is as bad as Columbus. But instead of stealing land he stole plots," the Chief said.

I ignored the comment.

"Cute pun." Mickey laughed.

"I do not pun."

"Like hell," I said. "Now let me say a word about the sources of drama in Elizabethan England."

"No," Chief Moses said.

"I'd like to use my education. I paid enough for it."

"Abuse it elsewhere," he said. "I do not care what you learned in drama at all of those schools you went to. Besides I read the play at FSU." He grinned. "Can I pass on the performance and go to the party?"

"No," Mickey told him.

According to St. John

"What part does Denny play?" I asked. "Not many female roles in *Macbeth* outside of the charming Lady herself."

"Must be a witch," the Chief said.

"You're right," Mickey said.

"I said I knew the play."

"It's not a bad part," I said. "You get to stir the cauldron and cackle."

The Chief grunted and sat down heavily on the couch.

"Are you going to go with us or not, Chief?" Mickey asked.

"Of course I am going," he grinned once again. "What do you take me for? A member of the Philistine tribe?"

My first partner was a mixture of bloodlines which he summarized as Florida Seminole mainly because the Indian family that raised him found him floating in a picnic cooler on the Tamiami Canal by a Seminole village. That's also how he got his name. Moses among the sawgrass blades.

When he got tired of wrestling alligators for tourists in the Everglades he left South Florida for L.A. He thought he could make it in the movies but found out he didn't fit any white director's image of an Indian. So like everyone else he pumped gas. But unlike everyone else he worked on cars too. Which was good considering the Chief's driving skills.

After his third accident in an L.A. parking garage he started back east. He made it to Vegas. He worked his way up from casino security, or bouncer, to running KENO games, Nevada's version of Bingo.

Then he took what he learned from the Vegas casino operation and parlayed it into consulting for Indian tribes setting up Bingo games on their reservations. The work paid well but he was losing interest. I got involved with him over three years ago when he came to Mendocino County to work with the Pomo Indians and their Bingo game. The Bingo setup was one of my first cases. What I got out of it was a check for services, a doctor's bill for a broken nose, and a partner.

"Now that tomorrow evening is settled can we get to work?" I asked.

"No," Mickey said as she sat down next to the Chief. She crossed her legs and tugged at the hem of her skirt.

"Why not?" I asked.

15

"Only if we get the video camcorder you promised. I know we've got the money," she said.

The camcorder became a real issue when Mickey started on another disability insurance fraud case almost two weeks ago. She didn't want to spend all of her time on a stakeout when a camcorder could do a lot of the work for her. She was reaching the limits of her patience. And we did have the funds. A month ago at the conclusion of our first murder case Rita Silverman came up with a substantial bonus for us for bringing in her ex-husband's killer. Unfortunately there were other demands on the money.

"I could send the Chief," I said. "And put you on the juror profiles." That was the kind of work Mickey hated, researching juries to give the defense an edge.

"Do not be an Indian giver, Jeremiah. The jurors are mine." Chief Moses was into researching juries. And finding people. What he didn't like was following someone around with a camera, waiting for an unguarded moment or a surreptitious visit to a motel.

"Now that's cute," I said.

"We'll go on strike. Just like the NFL players," Mickey threatened.

We were in the middle of the football strike of 1987 but this time the owners opted for replacements, fielding so-called scab teams. Unlike most fans I was looking forward to the Monday night scab game. I liked hearing about the jobs the replacement players had left for a moment of glory in the NFL—everything from teaching in college to driving a beer truck. There was even a P.I. on the Miami Dolphins.

"And you do not have the scabs to replace us," Chief Moses said.

There was only one way to resolve this. Ignore the other bills. Why pay old ones when you can run up some new ones? I would tap some of the Silverman funds and take a first step towards the high-tech modernization of our operation Mickey was always pressing for.

"What the hell," I said. "Go for it, Mickey. But would you make sure you get a good deal on the equipment?"

"I know what I'm doing, Jeremiah. But I'll take the Chief along to help negotiate. Sales clerks don't like to argue with him. They don't know what a pussycat he really is."

"Show me the treaty and I will sign, Long Knife." The Chief was into old westerns. Especially starring John Wayne.

"Now can we talk about computers in the office?" Mickey couldn't resist asking me.

"No," I said. "One concession at a time."

Mickey shrugged and stood up. "We'll see."

"So she and I go out in the field. But what the hell are you working on, Jeremiah?" the Chief asked as he rose from the couch.

It was another ritual. He knew I was working on that baffling case for the brokerage house and so did Mickey.

So I said: "Me? While you're out there busting your butts for the agency I've got to reread *Macbeth*."

2

The next evening we packed our entire agency into my black '56 Thunderbird coupe for the ride to the theater. It's the model with the louvered air vent on the hood, the porthole windows in the roof, and the spare tire mounted in steel and chrome behind the trunk. Along with the Corvette it was one of the two true American sports cars. Despite its vintage, it kept on running well thanks to the Chief's skill as a mechanic. I waited for, and got, the usual complaints about the size of the front seat from Mickey and Chief Moses.

"When are you going to get rid of this bomb and get something with a backseat?" Mickey asked.

"It could be worse. At least it's got a bench front seat." It was a tight fit but in 1956 the T-Birds had not yet gone to split bucket seats. We managed with Mickey in the middle, her legs turned away from the floor shift, her body mainly on the Chief's lap, and the Chief pressed up against the door.

I shifted into reverse.

"Will you watch my legs. I bruise easily," Mickey said as she shifted them to safety. "Damn this car!"

"Hey! It's a classic. At night it's nearly invisible. Like a Stealth Jet." I pulled out from a parking space on the street. There were already two cars, each coming from a different direction, ready to go to war over my vacated spot.

"So buy a bigger black one," the Chief said. This coming from a man who owned a King Cab pickup truck that was customized to just hold himself and a date.

"It's not just the color," I said.

"Stop fixing it for him, Chief," Mickey suggested. "Or screw up the engine next time like auto mechanics usually do."

Mickey spoke from experience. So much so that she no longer owned a car.

It was a new variation on an old theme and I ignored it.

Even though my partners were a little wrinkled from shoe-horning into the car they both looked elegant. Mickey was wearing a short teal blue dress cut low in front and back. It was a chilly evening and she wore a matching woolen cape over her shoulders. The Chief had finally bought a three-piece suit at the Long Man's Shop. It was dark blue with a subtle red pinstripe. A final touch was an extra long red paisley tie with his white button-down shirt. Compared to my partners I was dressed more casually in a camel blazer, rep striped tie, dark brown slacks, and oxblood loafers.

"You ought to buy a suit, Jeremiah," Chief Moses said.

My own words to him coming back at me—like spitting into the wind. But I had enough of suits in the years before I opened the detective agency. Besides, the blazers gave me a lot of room for my shoulder holster and my Smith and Wesson .38. Tonight, however, I wasn't carrying a gun. I didn't think I would need it to see Shakespeare. Someone else would have to take care of Macbeth in a more primitive way.

We went over the crest of the Franklin Street hill and down towards the bay. Below us the waters were spread in a blue black pool upon which floated the dark rock ship of Alcatraz. A great waste of valuable property I have always thought. Either reopen it as an escape-proof prison or turn it into a casino. Or let the Indians

According to St. John

take it over again and set up a Bingo game. With the help of Consultant Moses.

The Marina Theater was located by the water near the Marina Green Yacht Club. In contrast to the sleek yacht club buildings the theater was a large red brick structure that looked more like a warehouse than a theater.

We parked in the lot facing the massive silhouette of the Golden Gate Bridge. Amber lights hung like threaded beads across its span. Behind it the sky was dark but clear. The fires of summer that brought smoke in from the north were out and it wouldn't be until November that rain would come. October was its own brief separate season in the city.

As promised there were three tickets for us at the box office.

After we got them torn we passed into a foyer that ran in a semicircle around the entire orchestra. Across the foyer were two metal doors guarded by female ushers in black tuxedos.

One of them checked our stubs. We followed her down the left center aisle of the orchestra. Behind and above us was a large balcony. On each side of the theater were rows of private boxes at mezzanine level. There were gilded carvings on the front of each box and along the front wall of the balcony.

Mickey nudged me as we walked and tilted her head at a box to our left.

"That's Cleo Maura in the middle box," she whispered.

I looked up at the drama critic and saw a middle-aged woman wearing a large multicolored caftan with a long orange scarf wrapped around her neck and chin. On her head she wore a flamboyant wide-brimmed floppy hat that drooped over her forehead and obscured her face. With a hat like that she needed a private box.

"Imagine sitting behind her," I said.

"Those are her trademarks."

The Chief looked up. I felt sorry for whoever was going to have to sit behind him too.

"I never read her," he said. "I prefer the *Examiner* critic."

I read them all when I get the chance.

The usher handed us our programs and indicated the first three seats. I went in first, then Mickey, giving Chief the aisle. I prefer the aisle because I hate the feeling of being trapped, but size before beauty and paranoia.

Inside each program was a slip of paper on which was typed: "Tonight the part of Lady Macbeth will be performed by Denise Belknap."

"Your friend's stock has shot up," I said.

"My God! She told me she was Amanda Cole's understudy too. But . . ."

"I wonder what happened to Amanda Cole," I said. Miss Cole was a major San Francisco draw in previous years. And despite her recent decline it was her name that was supposed to bring the audiences in. Though the house was far from sold out tonight.

"A real break for Denny," Mickey said. "And with all the critics here for opening night." We glanced up at the box that held Cleo Maura.

"Very auspicious," I said.

"Or suspicious," the Chief retorted.

We both looked at him. As it turned out he was right.

The opening battle scene was typical Maydik casting. The good King Duncan was black, as was his son Malcolm. But his other son Donalbain was white and had a deformed leg. A character to watch out for. And of course Macbeth was white. Obvious color symbolism and hardly a surprise.

When the opening battle was won by Macbeth, three witches of indeterminate race appeared to predict his future. But there was a new twist to this appearance by the weird sisters. A fourth came out to join them.

"That's Denny," Mickey whispered, surprised.

Lady Macbeth, dressed as a queen, was playing one of the witches and tempting her husband to the throne of Scotland.

Denise Belknap, playing Lady Macbeth, was stunning. And tempting. She was tall, with long black hair flowing from under the crown she wore. Her face glowed white as porcelain with delicate features and high cheekbones. For the moment she was wrapped in royal sable. She looked every inch the kind of woman a man would kill for.

The actor playing Macbeth was listed as George Atwil. He was short, shorter than Denny, but well-built with a handsome leonine head and flowing thick brown hair and beard.

According to St. John

A murmur ran through the audience as it recognized the dual role Lady Macbeth was playing. I wondered how the critics would take Maydik's directorial device. I myself liked it a hell of a lot better than his color symbolism but what does a P.I. know—even one with theater training—about directing *Macbeth*?

As the action unfolded Denny manipulated her husband with her intense sexuality. When Macbeth hesitated to murder the king she questioned his manhood and made it clear that she would no longer sleep with him if he didn't come through with the crown. Faced with that dismal prospect Macbeth made his choice. What else could the poor guy do but knock off good old Duncan?

Right before intermission the witches reappeared but Lady Macbeth was no longer with them. She was now queen in fact, not fancy. I hoped Macbeth was happy with what he got in the sack in exchange for his soul.

When the house lights came up we made our way back up the aisle.

"What do you think of Denny?" Mickey asked.

I looked up at Cleo Maura's box and saw the critic get up and leave it.

"It's what the critics think that matters," I said.

"But what do you think?"

"I like her acting. And I like Maydik's interpretation."

"You can understand why the man did it," Chief Moses said.

"She had him by the balls," I concluded.

In the lobby a crew of caterers was setting up long buffet tables and hauling in trays of hot and cold food from a truck parked in front of the theater. Bottles of Korbel champagne went by packed in barrels of ice.

The three of us joined a crowd that went out into the street. A few people lit up cigarettes, fighting the raw wind from the bay with cupped hands and hunched backs. There were two San Francisco police cars in front and an orange and white ambulance parked at the side of the building. Barricades were starting to go up in the street. Across the side and back of the building yellow plastic strips that read: POLICE LINE DO NOT CROSS were stretched out.

"Wonder what the cops are up to?" I said. I didn't think they were here to protect the champagne and caviar.

"Not auspicious," the Chief said.

A tall bearded man in a black raincoat and fedora who was standing near us said, "I heard someone shot an actor."

"Which one?" I asked.

"Who cares? They were all lousy," the man said and disappeared into the crowd. I hoped he wasn't writing a review.

"What do you think happened?" Mickey asked me, acting as if I hadn't been sitting next to her in the theater for the last hour and fifteen minutes. She rubbed her hands together to keep them warm.

"You heard what that guy said."

"Come on," she insisted.

I jumped to an obvious conclusion. If Amanda Cole had to be replaced by her understudy . . .

I didn't say anything; I just looked at Mickey and the Chief. They had jumped to the same conclusion.

"Suspicious," the Chief said once again.

Instead of responding I offered to buy my partners some Perrier. Just then the lights in the lobby started going off and on, signaling us back into the building.

"No time for Perrier," I said.

"Perrier is out. Classic Coke is in," the Chief said.

"Not even time to use the powder room," Mickey complained.

Back inside the theater we had to displace three young men in fraternity blazers who were in our seats. I suggested that if they wanted to get up closer to the stage taking our seats wasn't the smart way to go about it.

"Must be the wrong row," one of them said as they checked out their ticket stubs and the Chief before retreating five rows back. Probably not their seats either but that wasn't our problem.

"Think they'll announce something on stage?" Mickey asked.

"About what?" I asked.

"Come on, Jeremiah! About whatever's happened!"

The curtain opened and she got her answer: No. It was boiling cauldron business as usual for the old hag witches.

"The show must go on," the Chief said.

"You learn that catchy phrase in Hollywood?" I asked.

"Do not remind me of your Tinsel Town, white man."

The Chief would always resent the casting practices that had kept him out of anything but crowd scenes.

According to St. John

"Sorry, red man. But it's not my town." And never would be if I could help it. I shared in the well-founded prejudice the northern half of the state felt for the hot and smoggy southern half. Once I even signed a petition for the creation of an independent state of North California. Nothing came of it because we have all the water and the south has all the thirsty people, swimming pools, and powerful politicians.

Mickey hushed us and we obeyed. Lady Macbeth had demonstrated the power of a woman already tonight. I didn't want to take a chance on what Mickey could do.

3

By Act V Lady Macbeth's conscience was really bothering her. She came on stage in a sleepwalk to wash out those damned indelible spots of blood from her hands. Only this sleepwalk, like a lot of other things in the production, was different. The only thing Denny was wearing was a candle.

The entire audience, including me, seemed to be in shock. This was not what you usually got when you went to see Shakespeare.

I glanced at Mickey and the Chief. Mickey was wearing a wide-eyed stare. The tip of her tongue was jutting out between her lips. The Chief's patrician jaw had dropped to his chest.

I quickly got back to Lady Macbeth. I tried to concentrate on the lines she was speaking but I was distracted, to say the least, by her nude body moving across the stage. She had high round breasts with small golden nipples, slim hips, and a thicket of pubic hair as black as the hair on her head. Her long hair could have covered her breasts but it hung straight down her back. No false modesty for the sleeping lady.

"To bed, to bed, to bed," was her exit line. It seemed to me that the stroll on stage had taken less than a minute but that was impossible. Time flies when you're watching a beautiful naked Lady Macbeth.

A buffoon in the balcony unleashed a wolf whistle and a few others followed. The rest of the audience, including the three of us, were coming out of shock. We tried to act blasé. Hell, *Oh, Calcutta!* was ancient theatrical history.

As Macbeth's enemies began to gather with drum and colors on stage, I whispered in Mickey's ear, "Can't you and your friends keep your clothes on?"

She turned slowly to face me with a wicked grin. "Are you complaining?"

"No."

"Not me," added the Chief.

The play plunged on to its conclusion with a black Macduff hauling in Macbeth's severed head. It was a good likeness of Atwil. The director was after authenticity from medieval sleeping habits to realistic decapitations.

The audience also got word that the fiendlike queen had rubbed herself out with her own violent hands. Offstage.

With the uxorious Macbeth disposed of, Macduff announced: "The time is free."

Maybe. Except for the white Donalbain limping unhappily around.

As the curtain fell Mickey asked no one in particular, "I wonder how Cleo Maura and the other critics are going to respond?"

I watched Ms. Maura rushing out. "We'll know soon enough."

The first curtain call was for the entire cast and the audience applauded enthusiastically.

We stood up and joined in the tribute.

When Denny took her solo bow there were a few more wolf whistles and some calls of: "Take it off, Lady Macbeth!"

"Jerks," Mickey commented.

Then the applause grew even louder, drowning out the jeers.

"Seems like they've forgotten Amanda Cole," I said.

"Cannot blame them," the Chief joked.

According to St. John

Mickey groaned.

When Denny came back on with Atwil there was a more sedate response.

The lights came up.

"Party time?" Chief Moses asked as he got up and turned in the direction of the lobby.

Mickey took his arm. "I want to go backstage. I want to see Denny."

We didn't argue with the lady.

We did argue with the uniformed cop who was guarding the stairs at the left side of the stage as we faced it. From the orchestra he had been hidden by the curtain. Now he was blocking our access to backstage. I read his name on the plate above his badge.

"Officer Hughes. We are personal friends of Lady Macbeth," I explained.

"I don't care if you're personal friends of William Shakespeare. Nobody gets back there. I got my orders."

He was about five ten and two hundred pounds. He had a ruddy Irish face that looked even redder from standing out in the wind. It was going to be tough to win an argument with him. Especially if he thought letting us by would get him sent back outside.

"What happened?" I asked as I tried to make my way up the steps to the curtain.

"Stay down there," he ordered.

"I've got to see Denise Belknap," Mickey said.

He wasn't impressed by Mickey's need.

The Chief just looked at him but Hughes wasn't impressed by the Chief's size. Not when he had the gun.

I was about to lead a strategic retreat to the lobby and the party when Detective Johnny Dajewski appeared.

"What's goin' on here?" he asked. Then he saw me and abruptly added, "Shit."

Detective Dajewski was a raw-boned Polish cop with boyish good looks and crayon yellow hair that made him look like a grownup Dennis the Menace. Everybody called him Johnny D., including his Mexican wife who after five years of marriage still could barely speak English. And Johnny D. was not exactly fluent in Spanish. Maybe that was why they got along so well.

The detective turned to go backstage.

"Johnny D.! It's me, Jeremiah." Like he didn't know.

He stopped with his back to me.

Johnny D. turned around and showed me the scowl on his face. I smiled in return.

"Whaddya want, St. John?"

"We need to talk to Denny Belknap," Mickey said.

"Oh you do?"

"Yeah." The three of us started up the steps.

Officer Hughes stepped forward to block our way.

Johnny D. gave it some serious thought. He took long enough to make me worried that he wasn't going to call off Hughes.

"Johnny?" I asked.

After a few more curses he came through.

"It's okay. Let 'em by."

"Thanks, Johnny."

"Sure," he said and shook his head.

Hughes glared at us as we passed but we ignored him. I wanted to treat the incident as nothing out of the ordinary for the St. John Detective Agency.

As we moved along a backstage corridor I asked, "This a Vice case, Johnny?"

"Maybe. Maybe not. But I got that transfer to Homicide."

So the Silverman case had given Johnny a career boost. He owed me one. No wonder he had let us go backstage.

On the other hand having Homicide cops backstage was not a good sign.

"Congratulations," I offered.

"This doesn't mean you get anythin' more outta me, St. John."

"Would I take advantage of our relationship?"

"Damn right."

"Since you put it that way, who died besides the Macbeths and their friends?"

"What's it to you? What's the Belknap woman to you?"

"She gave us comps," the Chief said.

"Why? 'Cause she heard what hotshot detectives you are? Figure you'd help solve the *Macbeth* case?"

"She was my roommate in college," Mickey explained.

Johnny D. stopped at the end of the corridor. He looked at

According to St. John

Mickey and said, "Oh? Nice dress." He added as he dropped his eyes, "It's . . . very . . ."

"Glamorous," the Chief said.

"And revealing," I tagged on. "It's not polite to stare, Johnny."

"You oughtta take your own advice," Johnny shot back.

I hadn't realized it but I was staring too. As though I'd never seen Mickey before. She had that effect on me, damn her. I stopped ogling by reminding myself that my P.I. trademark was subtlety.

Mickey didn't say a word.

We made a right turn into another corridor and stopped again after a few steps. To our right was a solid unbroken wall; to our left was a series of dressing rooms. I saw a Crime Scene Unit equipment cart parked outside the door of the middle room. I heard the whirr of a Polaroid at work.

"All right, Johnny. Who died?"

"Lady Macbeth, Jeremiah," he said.

"What?" Mickey asked.

"Amanda Cole."

We were stunned into momentary silence. Finally the Chief asked, "How?"

"Could be murder."

"What's the M.E. say?" I asked.

"He's gotta run some chemical tests."

I looked uneasily at Mickey. "You have a suspect?"

He hesitated. "Yeah."

"Who?" I asked.

"I can't say."

All I said was: "Sure you can, Johnny, you just open your lips. . ."

"Shit," he said but continued. "The other Lady Macbeth. The young one."

"No!" Mickey cried out. "Not Denny."

Her cry brought Detective Oscar Chang out of the middle room to stand in front of the CSU equipment cart. He looked like he was guarding it from us. As usual, he was dressed in a dark suit that looked fresh from the cleaners. Under his black, precisely parted, stiff hair his face was smooth as polished amber and taut as the tension he had to be feeling in his gut. His irises were bulging out like black marbles. He wanted to pitch the three of us the hell out of there but he had a problem: that same Silverman case. Chang had moved outside the law and ironically I ended up protecting him from the D.A. I could imagine the taste of ashes that left in his mouth. But it also left him reluctantly cooperative. It was nice to have friends in high places.

"What the hell are you doing here?" he called down the hall. The question was directed to me and my partners but it sent a message to Johnny as well.

"Hello to you too, Detective Chang," I said.

"We're here to see Denise Belknap," Mickey said.

Chang came down the corridor towards us. "She's busy," he said.

"What is she doing?" the Chief asked.

"She's going to be questioned."

"About a possible homicide?" I asked.

Chang looked angrily at Johnny D.

"With an attorney present?" Mickey asked.

"She doesn't want one."

"Sure. But does she need one, Chang?" I asked.

Chang shrugged.

"Jeremiah!" Mickey said.

"What?"

"You know."

I did. I thrust out my chest, cleared my throat, and announced, "I'm her attorney."

"Bullshit," Johnny ventured. "I thought you gave that all up. You're just a P.I. now."

I tried not to take offense at the way he said P.I.

Chang grinned. He knew some of my history. Before I opened the detective agency I was a deputy district attorney in one of the Bay Area's most crime-ridden counties.

I had gone into that office right out of law school loaded down with the baggage of idealism. I had to learn what they didn't teach in a classroom. What I saw in that D.A.'s Office was nearly everybody hustling to get out, looking for soft positions on special task forces, moving into less pressurized U.S. Attorneys' Offices, into well-paying criminal defense, or into private law firms that dealt

According to St. John

with everything from divorce to personal injuries. But I thought I could hang in there.

Then I made some very wrong moves in the office. I got involved with Sarah, one of the female prosecutors. She also happened to be the woman of choice of my immediate boss, a very well kept secret. Especially from me. The result was a career disaster.

I was given every case that was hopelessly deficient legally and potentially embarrassing to the prosecutor. After too many of those disasters I left to spend a year in a San Francisco personal injury law firm, dealing with the vagaries of whiplash and the intricacies of accident reconstruction. It was a year too much. But at least I met a few private investigators, got interested in the business, and made enough money to start my agency and buy a black '56 Thunderbird. I thought it was the kind of car a P.I. would drive in The City—as capitalized in the local newspapers.

Now here I was reclaiming my place at the bar. But this time it was for the defense of a very beautiful Lady Macbeth. And for a good cause, I hoped.

I told Chang: "I'm still an attorney in good standing before the California bar." I paused. "It's like the mark of Cain."

"Good analogy," was all he said, sparing me a demonstration of what he thought of as his sharp and unrelenting wit.

"Where is Ms. Belknap?" I asked.

"In another room down this hall." He turned abruptly and started walking away from us.

"Thanks," I mumbled to Johnny and couldn't resist adding, "You ought to take some style tips from Oscar. You still dress like you're in Vice."

"You keep this shit up my ass'll end up back there." He followed Chang down the corridor.

"You go play lawyer," Chief Moses said to me. "I am going to the gala opening night party as planned."

"If it's still on," Mickey said.

The Chief laughed. "This is show business, lady."

With Mickey in tow I started after the two Homicide cops.

4

I walked into a dressing room past a tall black cop who stopped Mickey at the door when Chang said, "Not the woman."

Mickey cursed and stood her ground but I couldn't think of any way to get her into the room just yet. The door closed behind me.

Denise Belknap was sitting on a stool with her back to one of the lighted oval mirrors that ran along each wall above the dressing tables. Her face was cleansed of theatrical makeup. The mirror made that delicate face look like it was framed in a cameo. She was wrapped in a blue satin dressing gown that she had pulled tightly around herself. The gown, as she sat, hung down almost to her ankles. The only thing bare about her now were her hands and feet. Offstage Lady Macbeth looked fragile and vulnerable.

In the P.I. business there is necessary and sometimes dirty work, from investigating accident victims for insurance companies trying not to pay off to tailing adulterers for other adulterers. This is the kind of work that pays the bills and lets the agency show a profit. Then there's the kind of work that makes you feel good about your calling, like getting ten grand back for an old widow on a pension who got caught in a version of the "Jamaican Switch" scam and couldn't get any help from the cops.

Helping Denny I put in this latter chivalric category. For now.

Oscar Chang, Johnny D., and I each pulled a stool away from the line of tables and sat down in a circle, with Denny at high noon. A piece of each of us was reflected in the row of mirrors behind her.

"Did you read Miss Belknap her rights?" I asked.

"Of course," Chang answered.

I turned to Denny and said, "You have the right to remain silent. Do it."

She screwed her mouth up. "Who the hell are you?" My maiden in distress didn't seem too friendly to her champion.

"That's what I'm always asking," Chang threw in.

"I'm Jeremiah St. John, your attorney," I told her.

"I don't need one, Mr. St. John." She sounded like she was telling a phone solicitor to go to hell.

"I told you," Chang said to me.

I ignored him and said to my reluctant client, "You never can tell."

"Are you the public defender?"

I was a handsome, clean-cut, thirty-one and she had taken me for an underpaid scruffy public defender. I figured she was feeling the pressure so I didn't take offense.

Before I could think of a snappy comeback, Mickey forced herself part way into the room. A black hand and a blue uniformed arm were reaching to haul her back.

"Denny!"

"Mickey!"

"What the hell is this?" Chang wanted to know.

"We haven't seen each other in years," Mickey called out as she struggled to hold her position.

"Do you know this guy?" Denny called to her old roommate. Meaning me.

"Let me go." Mickey was grappling with the black cop who was now beside her in the doorway.

"Let her go, Butler," Chang ordered.

According to St. John

Mickey brushed herself off, acting as if she had just got up from the floor after a brawl.

"This guy is your lawyer," she said to Denny.

"I don't need a lawyer. I don't like lawyers."

"Neither do I," I said.

Denny took a pack of Vantages out of a pocket in her robe. She tapped a cigarette and Johnny D. leaned over to light it with a disposable butane lighter. A class act. In my office I had a sign with a cigarette in a red circle crossed out by a red bar, but this was her space.

As if to emphasize her distaste for lawyers she blew smoke in my direction.

"I think you need a lawyer, Denny," Mickey persisted.

"Can I confer in private with my client?" I asked Chang.

"She doesn't seem to consider herself your client, St. John."

"Can't blame her for that," Johnny D. said.

"Good taste," Chang said.

"Denny! Will you listen to me?" Mickey pleaded.

"Do I have to"

"Damn right," she said.

"You gonna make up your mind?" Johnny D. asked.

Denny looked from face to face around the room. She settled on mine. She blew a ring of smoke to the ceiling and crushed out her cigarette. Then she turned to shut off the lights around the mirror.

"Damn you, Mickey." She hesitated then said, "Okay. Okay. I give up. He's my lawyer."

"Now can you leave us alone?" I asked.

"We wouldn't want to violate anyone's rights," Chang said as he and Johnny D. got up to leave.

"See you later," I said.

"Unfortunately a necessity." Chang waited for Johnny then closed the door behind them. It wasn't exactly a slam.

Mickey and Denny embraced wordlessly. Denny was about three inches taller than my partner's five eight. And her straight hair was about a foot longer. After a few moments of doing an awkward tango they released each other and sat down.

I got right down to business.

"If Amanda Cole was in fact murdered, what makes you a prime suspect?"

Denny shifted her weight. "Am I a prime suspect?"

"That's what I picked up from our police friends."

She took out the pack of Vantages and held it in her right hand.

"I can't say I'm that surprised," she said.

"Why not?" Mickey asked.

Denny crossed her legs and her gown hiked up. "We had a fight in my dressing room yesterday after rehearsal. Everybody in the cast and crew must have heard us going at each other."

"In here?" Mickey asked.

"No. In my dressing room. Down the hall."

"What's this?" I asked.

"A common dressing room. The police moved me in here to search mine."

"To search yours?" Mickey cried. "Can they do that? Don't they need a search warrant?"

"Mickey, you were a cop, remember? This is a crime scene. It's open season."

"And you said you didn't need a lawyer?" Mickey said.

Denny lit another cigarette and said, "I don't give a damn if they search. I don't have anything to hide."

"But you don't know what they're looking for," I said.

"How could I?" Denny asked. The burning cigarette was dangling from her fingers. She looked at it then took a deep drag. "I only know I didn't kill her."

"What about the argument?" I asked.

"She said I was trying to steal her part."

"Were you?"

"No."

"But you were the understudy. You wanted to play Lady Macbeth."

"I wasn't trying to steal her part. Not like she meant it."

"How was that?" I asked.

"By sleeping with Perry Maydik, the director."

"And you weren't?"

"No I was not," she said archly.

"But Amanda Cole believed it," I said.

"She came into my dressing room screaming like a banshee after I ran through the part. She accused me of sleeping with Perry to get her out. Then she said I was destroying the play for my own ends."

"Did she usually attend your run-throughs as her understudy?" I asked.

"She started last week."

"Why?"

"Because I was buying into Maydik's interpretation, which she hated."

"Is that what she meant by destroying the play?" I asked.

"Yes. That's what she thought. I thought his ideas were wonderful."

Some of them maybe, I thought.

Mickey brushed aside a stray hair and asked, "What exactly happened with her in your dressing room?"

"What do you think? I screamed back." Denny took a final drag and stubbed out the cigarette. "I told her she was too old to handle Perry's interpretation. That got her furious."

"Understandable," I said.

"Yes," Denny agreed. "But I was pissed off."

"Any violence?"

"She threw a punch at me."

"Missed?" I hoped.

"By a foot. I threw a makeup case at her."

"Missed?"

"It grazed her head. I guess it cut her. She ran out bleeding into the corridor and told everyone I tried to kill her."

"Who exactly is everyone?" I asked.

"Everybody in the cast and crew."

"That could work in our favor," I said. Anyone who knew about the incident would know how guilty Denise Belknap would look if something did happen to Amanda Cole.

"All right. So you had this argument . . . it doesn't prove anything," Mickey said.

"There's more."

There always is, I thought. "Such as?"

"I went to talk to Amanda tonight before I went on. Apparently I was the last person to see her alive."

"Except for the killer," Mickey said.

"That's understood," I said. "But why were you playing the part tonight? Did Maydik dump her?"

"She was sick."

"So she didn't want to go on?" Mickey asked.

"She couldn't. She was sick when she got to the theater this afternoon."

I pulled my stool up closer. I was watching the dark eyes, trying to read their expression. "What was wrong with her?"

"I don't know. But I've heard that she's always been high strung. That she had all kinds of food allergies. She'd never had a run without missing some nights."

"Makes the understudy especially important," Mickey said.

"And threatening. If the understudy is going to do a different interpretation," I added.

"Why did you go see her?" Mickey asked.

She fumbled for her cigarettes but changed her mind. "You want to know the truth? Because I was scared. Terminal stage fright. I was shaking all over. I never had a role like this before. I wanted to get some advice. And I wanted to make up with her. Forgiving trespasses and all that Catholic upbringing shit."

"And that's it?"

"Yeah."

"Did you make up?" I asked.

"I don't know. Amanda was still pretty out of it."

"What did she say?" I asked.

Denny hesitated. "She wanted to score some coke."

That gave us all pause.

"Did you give her any?"

"No. I don't have any of that stuff."

I looked at Mickey. She would know about Denny's college days' habits at least. To Denny I said, "If this is all Chang has it's just circumstantial."

"I don't understand about the coke," Mickey said.

"Neither do I. All I know is that she asked me if I had any."

"Did she ever ask you for coke before?"

"No. Never. But she sounded desperate."

There wasn't much more to ask.

"Okay, when our police friends ask you a question try to keep

According to St. John

your answer to a yes or no. If you have any doubts, confer with me."

"You're not bad for a lawyer," she said. "You haven't even mentioned your fee yet."

"Sounds like you had a bad experience."

"My divorce attorney."

"I didn't know you were married," Mickey said.

"Neither did my ex-husband. Not from the way he ran around on me."

I got up to open the door. "Actually I'm a P.I.," I said. "She's my partner."

"What? Is this a joke?"

"He's a lawyer too," Mickey assured her.

"Coming out of retirement just for you."

I got Detective Chang. He came back in with Johnny D. and said, "The Medical Examiner said it looks like Amanda Cole died of a drug overdose."

"Then Homicide won't be in on this one?" I asked.

"We are still here, St. John." He and Johnny D. reclaimed their stools.

Denny lit up another cigarette. This time she blew the smoke at Chang instead of me.

"Miss Belknap is awfully tired," I said.

Chang smiled without warmth. "Here or at the station house?"

"Here," I said.

Chang looked at Mickey. "You're not a closet lawyer, too, are you?"

"No."

"You'll have to leave."

Mickey went quietly out into the hall and Johnny D. shut the door behind her. I wondered if she'd join the Chief at the reception or wait in the corridor.

The questions from the two detectives were routine and repetitive. They kept coming back to the fight yesterday and the visit to Amanda's dressing room tonight. After the third repetitious run through, I asked, "Can we cut it off now? We're not getting anywhere. She's told you everything she knows."

"I appreciate your assurance," Chang said.

"Yeah," Johnny added in support.

It wasn't over yet. Chang bore in on Denny with those dark irises. "Do you use cocaine?"

"No."

Chang and Johnny both nodded. What the hell were they agreeing on.

"She can go," Chang said. "But I don't want her leaving town."

"She's got a play to perform in."

"I know, still. . . ." Chang said as the two detectives rose.

"Can I get my clothes from my dressing room?" Denny asked.

"The CSU is through," Johnny D. said.

"Sure," Chang concluded.

The two of them left us.

At least my client hadn't been arrested. That was something for a retired lawyer new to criminal defense.

Mickey hadn't gone to the reception. She was outside in the hall with the same Officer Butler who tried to remove her from the dressing room. Now they looked like they were busy flirting with each other. That's what I liked about Mickey. Always trying to improve our relations with the police.

We all escorted Denny to her dressing room. I noticed her name on the door which surprised me.

"We'll be a few minutes, gentlemen," Mickey said as she closed the door behind them, leaving Butler and me alone in the corridor.

"Heard any good ones lately?" he asked.

Spare me, I thought.

"I got one. You're not Mexican are you?"

"No."

"You hear about the Chinese an' their immigration problem? Thousands a Chicanos comin' into the country. Ever since they heard about two thousan' miles a wall with no writin' on it."

I laughed. "Chang tell you that?"

He rolled his eyes. "You a fuckin' loony, man. Detective Chang don't tell jokes. Not to a man in blue."

"Got any more?"

He was thinking about it when the two women came out sooner than I expected. Denise looked like she was dressed for a wake in a simple dark suit, a high-necked white blouse, dark stockings, and

According to St. John

low black pumps. I couldn't help but admire the two women, both beautiful, both so different in their looks. I could see it was one thing on which Officer Butler and I agreed.

The three of us left him to guard the empty dressing rooms while we walked along the corridors back to the wing where we had entered the backstage area. Officer Hughes was still on duty, looking like he was trying to think of a reason to stop us. He failed and let us by into the deserted theater. We could hear the noise of the party. I took each woman by the arm and led them out into the lobby.

The buffet must have been spectacular before the theater crowd got unleashed. There were remains of lobster tails and boiled shrimp, chicken wing bones, shishkabob sticks, and other evidence of elegant dining I couldn't recognize. There were some mangled pates, remnants of caviar molds, a few rare slices of beef heart, and some crusty sourdough bread, Swiss and Jack cheese, and cold cuts, including turkey, ham, and salami. In a chafing dish I found some Swedish meatballs and speared one with a plastic toothpick. It was passable. On a hot plate were some miniature hot dogs wrapped in pastry crust. I speared three of them with plastic swords and gave one each to Mickey and Denny. We dipped them into a nearly empty mustard dish.

At the end of one table there were a few thin slices of chocolate cheese cake and some strawberry tarts next to a fruit bowl of apples, pears, oranges, and grapes. I went over and got a grape cluster and started biting them off one by one from the bottom—very Roman orgy. They were seedless and sweet.

Each of the four tables had an ice sculpture as its shining centerpiece. On one of the two middle tables there was a large swan with upswept wings melting into a puddle that was designated as the Avon River on the base. Nice touch. The other middle table had a still-recognizable bust of Shakespeare. His bald crown glittered silver under the lobby lighting. The third table was adorned with Macbeth's castle—which looked more like a sand castle than a medieval one. It was melting neatly into its own moat. The fourth sculpture, melted almost beyond recognition, had once been a bust of Elizabeth I.

While action at the food tables was slowing down now that the locusts had been fed, the Korbel champagne was still flowing freely, courtesy of two crew-cut young men in red coats pouring away behind a portable bar.

It hadn't turned into a wake. The way the guests were acting they didn't seem to know that Amanda Cole was dead. Or they didn't give a damn. Had I missed the requisite moment of silence in memory of the late great actress? I would ask the Chief, if I could find him.

We penetrated deeper into the overflow crowd. I spotted the Chief across the lobby, his head high over what was left of some caviar. He was holding his own personal bottle of champagne.

Mickey went to him. She took him by the arm, ushered him over, and introduced him to Denny.

"Enjoyed your performance," he said without a hint of irony or trace of a leer.

"Thank you. I was nervous."

"I could not tell," the Chief said.

"Got your own bottle?" I asked him.

"Saves the boys a lot of pouring time. And me a lot of trips."

Someone in the crowd had started spreading the word that Denise Belknap was there. A lot of murmuring heads began to turn curiously towards Denny. Not a very subtle bunch.

Denny did her best to keep her cool.

"They know that Amanda Cole's dead?" I asked the Chief.

"Some gay announced it and said that the show must go on. That dearest Amanda would have wanted it that way."

"Like hell," Denny said.

Denny looked back over her shoulder. People were looking in her direction and talking among themselves. Their subject wasn't hard to figure out.

"I've got to get out of here," she whispered.

"Where are you staying?" I asked.

"I want her to stay with me tonight," Mickey said.

"Good idea."

"I don't want to be a bother. . . ."

"Don't be silly. We've got a lot to talk about," Mickey said.

Denny was very reluctant. She tried to beg off and I wondered why. But Mickey was persistent, so Denny finally gave in, but she didn't seem happy about it.

According to St. John

Since there wasn't enough room for four in the T-Bird, Chief Moses volunteered to stay on at the party. Tough assignment.

"There is a lady I met who would look good in a Seminole jersey," he told me.

"Good luck."

"Luck? What luck? This is Chief Moses here."

"Then to safe sex," I said as I took a swig from his champagne bottle.

The Chief would take a cable car to the office to get his pickup truck. Then he would drive across the city to his new unique accommodations. A houseboat on Mission Creek.

"Good night, Chief," Mickey said.

"It will be," he promised.

We went out through the main doors by the ticket booths past the police barricades into the cold night and around the side of the building to get to the car. The two women fit easily in the front and nobody made a comment. It was a short ride along the Embarcadero to Mickey's apartment north of the Ferry Building. On the way Denny told us how she had gotten this chance at the Marina while acting in a small Shakespearean repertory company in the valley after her divorce. Perry Maydik had come down from his summer home in Tahoe. He saw her, liked what he saw, and asked her to join his company a few months ago. She was living in a furnished apartment off Lombard, close as she could afford to the Marina.

Then she dozed off. I could see her face, pale and marked with lines of exhaustion, reflected in the windshield.

I pulled up in front of Mickey's apartment building. At two o'clock in the morning it was dark except for the bright lights in the lobby. Mickey got out her key and shook Denny awake.

After Mickey unlocked the lobby door, I walked them to the elevator.

"Tomorrow I'll get you a real attorney," I promised.

"You were great," Denny said as she took my hand and kissed my cheek lightly. "But I won't need one." She squeezed my arm.

I wanted her to be right, but knew she wasn't. "Goodnight ladies, goodnight, sweet ladies," I said as the elevator door closed on the two beautiful women. I was in love with both of them.

5

I got up just a few hours after I went to bed Wednesday morning. I expected Mickey and the Chief to be later than usual. It didn't bother me, since as partners they put in all kinds of unpaid overtime. But if they could hassle me about my car I could threaten to get a time clock for the office.

As for me, being on time was easy. I lived above the agency offices in the remodeled Stick-Eastlake Victorian we rented on Octavia Street in the Western Addition district of the city. The house was located near an area called Webster Hill, making us residents of a recently upgraded neighborhood with a recently created name. Which led to an increase in the rent. The house was close to the terminal point of the California Street Cable Car Line, which meant I could travel anywhere downtown and not have to take the T-Bird. Like other residents of the city, I used the cable cars for low cost transportation to downtown so I could avoid parking garages with their outrageous hourly rates. Only tourists rode them halfway to the stars.

Renting both floors of the Victorian gave me a convenient although expensive arrangement. The architecture with its angular features and its ornate square bay windows running the height of the building and even the dull blue with yellow trim that it was painted pleased my old-fashioned taste. It made me feel a part of the old city, the part that had survived the 1906 earthquake. That was how I liked to think of myself, as part of a great tradition.

I had a bedroom, a bath, a kitchen, a small living room and a back porch with a view of my neglected backyard.

I had converted the second bedroom into my personal gym, complete with weights, rowing machine, exercise bicycle, locker—with Mickey's *Playboy* picture hanging up in it—and basketball court.

The Victorian was the only building I could find that had ceilings high enough to allow me to raise a glass basketball backboard and hoop to the regulation ten feet. For me basketball was the only real game and to play it indoors I needed high ceilings and an entire house to myself. Downstairs neighbors wouldn't understand my passion as it reverberated through the house.

My gym floor was parquet and the polished light and dark woods made it look like the Celtics' court at Boston Garden, which I liked even though I am a diehard Warriors fan.

I dressed in gray cotton sweats for a workout. The office downstairs was locked and the answering machine was on. The world and even the city wouldn't stop if I opened up late this morning.

It would have to be a light workout. The Chief and I had taken up playing one-on-one basketball and when it came to a physical confrontation my finesse, dexterity, and skill, all compressed into a six-foot-one, one hundred seventy-five pound body, were no match for the raw force of the six-seven, three hundred pound Chief. In a struggle over a rebound a month ago I wrenched my back trying to hold on to a ball that Chief Moses was determined to have. He won. The injury forced me out of the City League this season. Last year I had played on a mixed team—P.I.'s and lawyers—called the Deadbeats.

I spent twenty minutes on the exercise bicycle and then lifted weights, running through only one set of repetitions of each lift. I

According to St. John

spent a half hour on the court shooting layups and jump shots. When I quit my back was sore. I shaved and showered. Then, wrapped in a towel, I went into the kitchen and fixed myself a bowl of Wheaties with milk and sliced banana. The box had a picture of a Denver Bronco on it.

The Victorian had a good-sized kitchen with ancient but functioning appliances and I did occasionally cook a meal. But as a rule I preferred eating out. Or sending out for Chinese or pizza.

The refrigerator was well-stocked with Henry Weinhard's beer in dark brown bottles. For me beer from an aluminum can is almost as bad as a wine cooler out of anything. But I couldn't convince the Chief, for whom I always had to keep a couple of six packs of Budweiser on ice. For Mickey it was a bottle of chilled Sonoma County white wine.

As I dressed Mickey came in.

"I'm here, Jeremiah," she called up to me.

The agency was open for business—and only a little after ten.

When I came down she was in the front room that doubled as her office and the reception area going through her morning ritual of makeup repair. A redundant ritual if ever there was one. This morning she was wearing an oversized blue and green novelty sweater and black slacks.

"How's Denny doing? She up yet?" I asked.

"Up and gone. She took a cab to her apartment early this morning. She was anxious to get back."

I thought about how reluctant Denny had been last night to stay with Mickey. Something was bothering me, but I put it aside.

"Think we'll see the Chief this morning?" I asked.

"Probably worn out from last night."

"He's going to have to order some new FSU T-shirts."

Mickey dug around in her cosmetic bag. "Do you still think Denny needs a lawyer? She was pretty adamant about not wanting one this morning. She doesn't trust them."

"Who does? But she needed one last night."

"That was only you."

"Thanks."

"There is one other problem. Money to pay a lawyer. Denny told me she's just about broke."

"So you recommended a public defender?" I asked.

"No. I told her not to worry about it."
"That was sisterly of you. So the bills will get sent to you?"
"I guess. If she has to have one."
"She does."

I would try to work out something better for Denny and Mickey but I wasn't sure what.

"Who are you going to call?"

Given the circumstances I gave that one some thought.

"I'm going to call Forsander and Samaho."

"But we've never worked with them," she said. She got out a bottle of salmon-colored nail polish and started painting her nails. It was better than lighting up a cigarette—the habit she recently broke after a year of my badgering.

"That's why I'm calling them."

Scott Forsander and Brian Samaho were law partners who played with me on the Deadbeats last season. Scott was a six-foot-six WASP—almost as tall as the Chief but a hundred pounds lighter—and Brian, a Japanese-American who claimed to be five-three but no one believed him. Scott was Mr. Inside and Brian was Mr. Outside with a deadly accurate jumper from beyond the three-point line. I alternated between point guard and short forward. I missed the league this year.

"That's crazy," Mickey said as she stroked a nail with the tiny brush.

"No, it's not. Would you want her to be represented by anyone we've worked for?"

"The ones in or out of prison?"

"Besides, I played basketball with them."

"Is that supposed to be a recommendation?"

"You can learn a lot about a lawyer on the basketball court."

"Like what?" She blew on her nails.

"Unlike most of the attorneys in the league they don't threaten to sue if they get hit by an illegal blow."

"That's not necessarily good."

"Yes it is. They don't threaten. They get mad and score and win."

"How do you tell if a female attorney is any good?" She closed the bottle of polish.

"And I thought you were going to do your toes next."

According to St. John

"This is an office. And you're avoiding my question."

"Same way. By how she plays ball."

"Men!"

I ignored that and left Mickey at her desk admiring her salmon nails. I passed through the Chief's middle office and went back into mine. The three-in-a-row arrangement worked well for us. It kept us separated just enough. There was a hallway that ran along outside of the offices and the Chief and I had side doors through which we could escape. In the hallway were the stairs that led up to my living quarters. Under the stairs the attorney who had previously rented the Victorian had put in a small but modern bathroom. The attorney had to vacate the building and give up his practice to serve time for conspiracy to distribute cocaine. He should have gotten himself a good drug lawyer.

I called the firm of Forsander and Samaho and got a secretary who put me on hold. I listened to the Beach Boys singing "Rhonda" until Scott Forsander came on the line.

"You cut into one of my favorite songs," I complained.

"We change the tape once a week," Scott said. "It soothes upset clients. You want to go back on hold to hear the rest of it?"

"I have the album so I'll pass. How are we doing in the league this year?"

"Don't you check the *Chronicle*'s 'Sporting Green'?"

"Come on."

"We've dropped a few. We could use you, man."

"Nice to be appreciated but I'm out of it this year. I'm not even on the Deadbeat roster."

"How's the back?" he asked.

"Getting there. I'm working out again."

Scott said, "I don't think you called for a local sports update, Jeremiah. What is it?"

"Did you hear about Amanda Cole?"

He had read about her death in the morning newspaper. I told him about Denny and my part in it.

"Now I need a real attorney for Denise Belknap."

"Why me?" he asked.

"Not you in particular. Either you or Brian." I explained my lawyer and basketball theory to him.

"Makes sense," he said.

"Then you'll pick up where I left off?"

Silence. "Let me look into it. Let me talk to her. Then I'll get back to you."

"Soon."

"Yes. I've got to talk to Brian. This isn't what we usually do."

"I know."

I hung up and buzzed Mickey on the intercom.

"Would you get Denny on the phone and tell her to call Scott Forsander."

"Is he going to take the case?"

"He's considering it."

"What did you tell him?"

"The truth." I cut us off. I turned in my chair to look out the window. I found myself thinking of how vulnerable Denny Belknap had looked last night during the interrogation. I hoped I was getting her the right attorneys.

I looked over the juror reports that the Chief had filed and took care of some correspondence. Then I gave some thought to the stock fraud case I was working on. As usual, the brokerage house didn't want an embarrassing police presence and the bad publicity. So they had hired a P.I.

I began to doze off. My short night of sleep was catching up to me early. I went into the Chief's office where we kept the Mr. Coffee machine and got the glass pot.

Mickey was at her old IBM electric typewriter. It was the machine she wanted to replace with a MAC computer.

I got some water from the sink in the bathroom, filled the top of the coffee maker, and pushed the on button, without even looking at the instructions once.

"Want some coffee?" I asked.

"Always, except when Chief makes it."

Chief Moses made his so-called Everglades coffee by pouring in three times the required amount of ground coffee and half the required amount of water.

Mickey and I were sitting on the couch in my office drinking passable cups of coffee when we heard the unmistakeable sounds of the Chief's arrival.

"Where is a P.I. when you need one?" he called out.

"Back here on a coffee break," Mickey shouted.

According to St. John

Chief Moses came into my office with a giant silver and black Oakland Raiders mug filled with coffee. He took a chair, reversed it, and sat down in front of my desk. He looked groggy. He was wearing the pants and shirt from last night but not the vest, jacket, or tie. He took a sip and made a crack about weak coffee.

"Hope you didn't overdo it and sink your houseboat," I said. The Chief's houseboat had a sign on it that read: "If It's Rocking Don't Bother Knocking." It hung right above the "No Solicitors" sign.

Chief Moses grunted. "No such luck." Then he gave me his usual complaint of these days. "The white man is ruining casual sex. This woman was an AIDS hysteric. She is even afraid of doorknobs."

"Depends on what you do with them," I said.

"You should have shown her your negative test results for the HIV virus," Mickey suggested.

"I did. But she said that they were out of date. No sex and she took a jersey."

Mickey got up. "I'm going back to work. I've had enough of this adolescent conversation."

"I need some sleep," the Chief said. I got up and let him lie down on the couch.

In ten minutes he was snoring and I couldn't get any more work done. So I decided to do a little investigating into the Amanda Cole case.

I waved goodbye to Mickey without answering her question about where I was going. I decided to take the T-Bird to the precinct house, which had visitor parking spaces.

Unfortunately, those were all taken up by illegally parked police cars and I had to park two blocks away in a Burger King lot for patrons only.

At the precinct house I went through the double main doors and passed through a metal detector. In anticipation of this security check I had left my Smith and Wesson back at the office. The police didn't appreciate visitors with concealed handguns on their turf. But how would they handle security when the new undetectable plastic handguns made the metal detector obsolete?

I went into the muster room on the main floor and up to the sergeant who sat behind a desk that rose as high as a judge's bench. An American flag was in a stand on his right, a California state flag in a stand on his left. There was a picture of the soon-to-be-departing woman mayor behind him.

Johnny D. had started out downstairs, in the bowels of the building, with Vice. That division was next to Narcotics which was next to the police locker rooms and showers, the toilets, and the basement holding cells. Now he had moved up to the second floor to Homicide, which shared space with Robbery and Burglary. The second floor also housed the interrogation rooms, clerical support, and administration offices.

After eying my I.D. long enough to read the information on it twenty times, the desk sergeant, a heavyset gray-haired cop in his fifties, signed me in and gave me a clip-on visitor's badge. Then he directed me to the stairs at the back of the room. I nodded at him and walked past a bulletin board of wanted posters—to which some precinct clown had added a copy of a WANTED–DEAD OR ALIVE–BILLY THE KID poster—and up a flight of metal steps.

Johnny's transfer to Homicide hadn't improved his working conditions much—except that the Homicide detectives had large dirty windows to try to look out of. Johnny was at a desk out in the middle of the division bullpen. Still no private space. I saw Detective Chang's glass-enclosed office. He wasn't in it, which was fine with me.

I made my way through the maze of desks to Johnny. When I got to his desk he said without looking up from the report he was typing with the classic hunt and peck method, "My kid broke a finger this mornin' and my wife banged up the car drivin' to the doctor. I hear bad things come in threes," he said as he struck a key. "Hello, Jeremiah."

"Nice change of scene. I like the windows," I said, ignoring his wise-ass comment.

He stopped typing and looked at a window. "Same old shit."

"I thought you wanted out of Vice."

"Yeah. I did. Like I said it's been a bad mornin'. I just got in."

"Can you answer a couple of questions?"

"I work for the city. Not the St. John Agency."

"You answer and you can get back to work for the city."

"Christ. What now?"

"How was Amanda Cole killed?"

"Didn't get the M.E. report yet."

According to St. John

"Does it look like murder?"
"We're waitin' for the final report."
"You taking lessons from Detective Chang?"
"Maybe."
"At least tell me who discovered the body."
He hit a few more keys then said, "The director, Perry Maydik."
"Is Denise Belknap a real suspect?"
"Hell does that mean?"
The phone rang. He picked it up and said "Yeah" a half dozen times then hung up.
"That was Chang. I gotta meet him. There's a break in the case," he said as he got up and moved away from his desk.
I repeated my question about Denny.
"Yes."
I tried to get him to explain as I followed him out of the building but I couldn't get another word out of him. The man was learning from Detective Chang. He pulled away in one of the illegally parked cars, leaving me standing alone on the pavement.
I decided to go get a Whopper.

6

Late that afternoon I was alone in the office when Scott Forsander called.

"This is more complicated than I thought," he said.

"Why?"

"Denise Belknap is under arrest."

"What?"

"They arrested her at her apartment. She called me from the Hall of Justice."

"Good work so far, Scott."

"Hey, the police moved fast."

"Why aren't you down there?"

"Brian was at the Hall on another case. He's with her."

"What's the charge?"

"First degree murder."

"Damn."

"Come down to my office. We've got to talk. And bring your cute partner."

"Which one is that?"

"The one who doesn't wrestle alligators."

"Sorry. They're both out on assignment."

The Chief was in the final stages of a pre-employment background investigation of a possible new VP for one of the city's largest banks. He had finished the phone checks and the credit checks and now he was doing a little pavement pounding. Mickey was out reviewing the video tape that recorded the movements of our disability fraud suspect.

"And you're sitting there on your ass with nothing to do?" he asked.

"I'm on my way." I slipped the S&W revolver into the holster under my gray blazer. Attorneys couldn't be as touchy as cops about weapons on their turf.

I took the California Street Cable Car to Forsander and Samaho's office in a high-rise tower on Montgomery.

I rode the elevator up to the tenth floor and followed the arrows that pointed to 1010. Forsander and Samaho had their names in gold leaf on a solid wooden door. No frosted pebbled glass these days.

The receptionist, a stocky Oriental woman, was at a desk in the waiting room. Unlike some attorneys—notably drug lawyers I have worked for—Forsander and Samaho didn't have an elaborate security system. There was no metal detector, no electronically controlled doors, and no bulletproof glass booth for the receptionist.

I gave her my card.

She wore her black hair short around one of those round faces that didn't reveal age or emotion. She glanced at the card and said as she rose, "This way please." She led me to Scott's office.

Forsander got up to shake my hand. He looked like something out of *GQ*, especially to someone accustomed to seeing him in a basketball uniform. He had on a lemon-colored shirt, a darker yellow tie, and gold suspenders. The vest and jacket of his dark blue suit were hanging on a coat rack in the corner. He wore his blondish hair long, out over his shirt collar.

His well-appointed office had a solid oak desk and comfortable leather chairs. There was a large red and gray Oriental rug on the

According to St. John

floor and about a dozen bonsai trees around the room. Scott had covered the walls with his framed law degrees and about forty pictures of himself playing basketball or posing in a team picture in a variety of uniforms from high school to college to semi-pro to Italian. Scott had played briefly for an Italian professional team before giving up completely on the NBA dream. I looked for our City League team picture then remembered that none of us Deadbeats showed up to have it taken. On his wastebasket hung a miniature backboard, hoop, and net for shooting crumpled papers.

"This a law office or a jock's den?" I asked.

"Talking sports trivia puts a client at ease."

"Not when you're charging by the minute."

Scott had an unobstructed view of San Francisco Bay through the picture window behind him. I looked at the Oakland Bay Bridge, and the hills above the East Bay city. It was a day so clear the sky seemed scoured to an unnatural silver blue.

There was a small No Smoking sign discreetly placed on Scott's desk. My kind of lawyer.

"Have a seat."

I did.

"Want a drink?" Scott swung open a cabinet that held an assortment of liter liquor bottles and a mini-refrigerator. "I've got ice."

I looked at my watch. Almost late enough. But not quite. I shook my head.

He closed the cabinet without getting anything for himself and sat down behind his desk. He looked concerned.

"Something bothering you, Scott?"

"We don't specialize in criminal law," he said.

"You've handled cases."

"Sometimes. But not murder."

"Are you saying you don't want to do it?"

"I'm telling you up front there are more high-powered criminal attorneys in town."

"I know. I've worked for them. That's why I'm here."

He thought that over.

"I don't know," he finally said.

"But I do, Scott. I want you on this one."

He nodded and pulled his suspenders forward with his thumbs. A skinny Clarence Darrow.

59

"All right. We could take the case. But there's another problem."

"I can't wait to hear this," I said. I knew what was coming.

"Your friend is so broke she could qualify for a public defender."

"No kidding?"

"Don't play dumb with me, Jeremiah."

I wasn't going to tell him about Mickey's offer. I had other blandishments.

"This is a big case with a lot of newspaper coverage. The publicity alone will make it worth it for you."

He crumpled up a piece of stationery and took a shot at the miniature basket. It went right through the net and into the wastebasket. "I've got a partner to feed," he said.

"Only one."

"Yeah. But don't let his size fool you. He's a hungry sonofabitch."

"It'll be worth it."

Scott thought it over.

"We could use the publicity. I admit it."

"So? What's the problem? Besides money?"

He hesitated. "We'll take the case on one condition. We're going to need your help."

"For what?"

"For the defense investigation."

I laughed. "Without the customary fee, of course."

"You work as our investigator on this and we represent your Denny Belknap. The barter system. Services for services."

"Okay. But I want some real business sent our way when this case is done. I've got *two* hungry partners to feed."

Scott stood up and walked around to the front of his desk.

"Okay. You work as our investigator on this and I'll send you enough clients to keep your partners in filet mignon or veal Oscar or beef Wellington or whatever they eat."

I smiled. Now we were getting somewhere. Thanks to good ol' basketball networking.

We shook on it.

It was ironic. Usually the Chief and I fell for the charity cases while Mickey would remind us that we had a business with a bottom line to run. A business with a lot of high-tech equipment

According to St. John

needs. Now it was Mickey's turn to put us in the red with her former roommate. At least for now.

"How about that drink now?" Scott asked.

"It's late enough. I'll have some Wild Turkey on ice."

We eyed each other over glasses of 101-proof bottled-in-bond bourbon and ice. The booze felt pleasantly warm in my throat and gut. We finished our drinks without saying anything and he poured us each another. I put mine down on the floor to let the ice melt a little more. I wanted to hear whatever else Scott had to say while my head was reasonably clear.

He took out a set of notes from a desk drawer.

"We got the M.E. report. Apparently the coke found in her system had been cut with a new cocaine helper."

"Which was?"

"Just another white powder. Potassium cyanide."

"Sounds harmful to your health."

"Class-six stuff. Super deadly. It can kill you in minutes. Seconds if you're lucky."

I took a swallow of the Wild Turkey. This was only going to get worse. "Who has this kind of shit lying around?"

"Anyone into electroplating, fumigating, gold and silver mining, photo processing, etc."

"But why arrest Denny?"

Scott held his drink up and looked at it. "Brian said traces of the tainted coke were found on Denny's dressing table hand mirror. The cops think she cut the cocaine with cyanide right there."

"Ties in perfectly with the fight on Monday and the visit to Amanda Tuesday night."

"You've got it," Scott said. He drank the bourbon down in a single gulp. To hell with admiring it.

"How do the police think Denny got Amanda Cole to snort this stuff?"

"Right before Denny went in to see her she tried to score some coke from two members of the crew."

"But no luck," I said.

"No luck. And then Denny comes along and the next thing you know she's snorting lady cyanide."

"Like Denny said, she was there to make peace. A little coke makes a pretty good peace offering," I said. It was easy to see where the police were coming from. "Okay. But is there anything else to connect Denny to the cocaine?"

"Off the record, Brian heard from a contact that the police have a Candy Man who swears he sold some coke to Denny Belknap on Sunday."

"What did Denny tell Brian?"

"She admitted it."

"So she's into coke." She had lied to me. Not a good start. "Does she still have the stuff? We can have a lab run comparison tests, cobalt thiocyanate, the brighter the blue the higher the grade, or chlorine, for the red trail, to see if it was cut with a synthetic. It may turn out to be a different batch from the tainted coke."

"You know your shit. Unfortunately she flushed it this morning. She was worried about the cops coming over to her place and finding it."

No wonder she didn't want to stay with Mickey last night. No wonder she was in such a rush to get back this morning.

"That wasn't too smart."

"If you assume it wasn't the same batch."

Scott was right. We were not necessarily working for an innocent person.

"Conflict over the part: motive. Cocaine: means. The visit to Amanda: opportunity. Plus the witnesses. Anything else? Did the cops find a barrel of potassium cyanide in Denny's pantry?"

"Not yet."

"What the hell. They don't have a case."

We each had another shot of bourbon. Outside the silver sky was beginning to darken to slate.

I had forgotten all about the reviews of *Macbeth*. After I left Scott's office I stopped at a combination flower shop and newsstand on Clay and bought copies of every San Francisco newspaper, morning and evening editions.

I tried to read the reviews on the cable car but it was too crowded to open the pages up. I settled for scanning the sports headlines. It looked like this year's football strike was just about over. The Warriors' November season opener was less than a month away. I would have to get my tickets soon.

When I got back to the office Mickey and the Chief were still

According to St. John

out. I started on the reviews. One reviewer for a morning newspaper loved Denny and the nude sleepwalk but was disappointed in Atwil's performance, a second reviewer thought Atwil was brilliant and Denny less so but he was enthusiastic about the authentic touch of the sleepwalk, a third reviewer for an evening paper found both of them too sexually intense and the nude sleepwalk gratuitous exploitation. They all commented favorably on Maydik's color-blind casting. All of them of course paid tribute to the late Amanda Cole.

I saved Cleo Maura for last. She was the most negative of them all. She panned Denny's performance and those of most of the supporting cast. Atwil had been weak, she speculated, because he didn't have Amanda Cole to rely on. And then she went on at great length about the great loss that the world of theater had suffered by Amanda's untimely death. To her, Denny was not worthy to take on the role of Lady Macbeth. Cleo Maura did not like Maydik's sexually intense interpretation and particularly berated him for the naked sleepwalk. No accounting for taste. She also disliked the unconventional but too obviously symbolic racial casting.

In general the other critics had praised Maydik's approach and all of them had thought his having Lady Macbeth be one of the witches tempting Macbeth inspired. Maura was strangely silent on the latter subject. But then she wasn't that interested in talking about Denny Belknap.

I was clipping the reviews out when Mickey and the Chief came in.

"Leave him alone and he starts cutting out paper dolls," Mickey said.

"These are *Macbeth* reviews." I passed them what I had cut out and they took them over to the couch to read.

Mickey asked me, "What do you think?"

I wasn't giving up on her yet. " 'Whoever loved who loved not at first sight?' " I quoted.

"Indian wedding chant. Also singles bar pickup line," the Chief contributed.

"Jeremiah," Mickey said, "I was asking about the reviews. Not Denny's effect on your adolescent hormones."

"I think she's got lots bigger problems than some mixed reviews."

The Chief rose. "Let us talk about it over dinner."

The man had a look of serious hunger on his face. We went to dinner.

We walked five blocks up Nob Hill to the Hyde Street Grille. It was a clean, no-frills place with formica tables, plain whitewashed walls, and large windows that let in a lot of light. The menu ran from hamburgers and steaks to great native specialties of the Pakistani chef. And the prices were right.

I ordered a Henry's, Chief Moses a Bud, and Mickey a glass of white wine from the Indian waitress who had appeared instantly at our table.

She came back with the drinks and a blackboard with the menu on it. I went for the chicken tikka, broiled chicken slices in a hot sauce served with grilled onions. The Chief went for chicken curry which came with a garlicky fruit sauce. Mickey was on a diet as usual and went for a low-cal Pakistani version of a Cobb salad which lacked most of the usual ingredients.

The waitress rushed off with our order and I ran through what had happened today.

"Are you sure Forsander's okay?" Mickey asked.

"I'm sure. Hell, he's not charging Denny or you."

"I'm afraid you get what you pay for."

"Not in this case. I told you. . . ."

"Don't give me that basketball bull again. This is my friend we're talking about."

"It's not free. We're bartering services."

"You two don't mind?" Mickey asked.

"No, woman," we said together.

"I appreciate it." She kissed us each on the cheek.

I didn't mention the deal about Scott sending us new business. I'd save that.

"What about bail?" she asked.

"It hasn't been set." I drank my beer.

"Can they deny bail?" she asked.

"In a murder case they sure can."

"And how will she get the money to put up anyway?" Chief Moses asked as he picked up his can of Bud. In all of our concern about the attorney's fee we hadn't given much thought to bail.

According to St. John

I looked at Mickey.

"If I have to," she said softly.

I didn't know how to negotiate that one.

We drank in silence until the Chief said, "There is another question here."

"I know," Mickey said.

I looked at her. "What about Denny and drugs?"

She shook her head. "Never back in college. But that was a long time ago."

"Did she say anything to you last night?"

"About what?"

"Drugs."

"No."

"We will have to see what else the police come up with," Chief Moses said.

"Unfortunately," I concluded.

Our dinners arrived. We ate in silence.

Halfway through the Pakistani chef appeared.

He leaned over our table and asked, "How is everything?"

"The food is fine," I said.

A few other things were not, but that wasn't his problem.

A well-fed but worried trio left the grill.

7

My Thursday morning plan was to begin my defense investigation with a re-creation of Amanda Cole's last twenty-four hours. After that I would concentrate on the twenty-four hours following the murder. Out of those two days I hoped to get something to break the case in a different way from the police—who had broken it like an egg on top of my client.

I would talk to the director, the cast, the crew, the box office staff, the house manager, the custodians, and anyone else who could help to reconstruct Amanda's movements. But first I wanted to hear what the police came up with.

I called Johnny D., who was out, and I left a message for him to call me back.

Mickey was at her desk out front. The video camcorder was back in operation at her high-tech stakeout by the Lake Merced singles complex. Chief Moses was organizing his files which he liked to do at least once a month. He was through with the pre-employment check. The candidate for the bank VP job turned out to have two wives. One in Berkeley and one in the city. Not much chance for that candidate despite his good credit rating.

While I waited for Johnny D. to return my call I started typing my reports on prospective jurors. After my fifth mistake on the same page I cursed the old electric machine as I reached for the bottle of Rembrandt opaque white correction fluid. Mickey was right. We needed word-processing equipment. But I wasn't going to give her the satisfaction of admitting it—yet.

I escaped from typing when Mickey led a stunning redhead into my office. Usually they call first but this was walk-in-off-the-street trade.

When she took off her coat a clinging green knit dress revealed a stunning figure as well. She sat down and crossed her legs. She had freckles on her thighs.

"I want my son back," she began softly as she took a handkerchief out of a large leather purse and dabbed at her eyes. She was careful not to wipe the mascara from her lashes.

Her ex-husband Harry Slater had disappeared two months ago with their only child after a bitter custody battle which he lost. After two months the police had nothing. She wanted something done. And she had the money to pay for it.

I called in the Chief and introduced him as the Great Seminole Tracker.

She nodded her head and looked pleased. She provided a sketchy history and the names of a few friends and one girlfriend. Not much to help the Chief find the bastard. There were possibilities from Key West to Honolulu.

"And when you catch up with him bust his ass," she said as she dabbed her eyes again. Then she left.

The Chief was going to enjoy this.

I went back to typing, Rembrandt correction fluid, and swearing. Finally Mickey took pity on me or couldn't stand my cursing anymore.

"You sit at the reception desk," she said as she took over.

"Fair exchange."

Before I could do anything else the phone rang. I took the call and tried to sound as sexy as Mickey.

According to St. John

It was an aide to a political candidate in the upcoming city elections. She wasn't impressed with my voice. She just wanted me to dig up some dirt on a certain supervisor. It was as blunt as that. I looked at our calendar and current clients and decided I could have the luxury of ethics and turn this one down. Besides I wasn't much interested in the election. Except for the vote on a new downtown stadium. Keep the Giants in San Francisco.

I gave her the name of a competent friend who needed the business and hung up. I knew that if I were in his place I would take the job. Situational ethics and I were no strangers.

I took the file for my stock fraud case and spread it open on Mickey's desk. I thumbed once again through the copies of the accounts the brokerage house had provided. I separated the accounts according to profitability over the past year. Five of them seemed remarkably profitable with almost all of the profits coming from trading the Standard & Poor's 500-stock index futures. And all were with the same broker. I had something to suggest to my client. That we set a trap.

It was nearly noon and I was getting hungry when Johnny D. returned my call. It didn't impress him that I was answering my own phone.

"I'm pissed off," he announced.

"Why?"

"Don't leave me Goddamn messages to call you! You know what that makes me look like? Huh?"

"My errand boy?"

"Shit!"

"How else will you know to call me?"

"Use your damn P.I.'s brain. If you got one."

"Next time I'll say call Travis McGee."

"Fuck you."

"How about Hoke Moseley?"

"What the hell's a Hoke Moseley?"

"You ought to keep up with your reading. He's the model cop of the 80's."

"I'll wait for the movie."

"Chang saw the message?" I knew what had pissed him off.

"Picked it up right off my desk. Gave me his worse evil eye."

"Sorry."

"Whaddya want anyway? Let's get this over with."
"Amanda Cole's last twenty-four hours. Your reconstruction."
"Can't you do your own scut work?"
"Sure. But this way I can compare notes."
"St. John, you know I can't . . ."
"Nothing that won't come out anyway. You're just saving me some time. You've got to be fair to the competition."

That was only partly true. If you're the defense you don't have to be fair. The laws of discovery in California are a bad joke to prosecutors who have to reveal their witnesses in advance. For them it is more like trial by ambush. And I was ambushed enough myself while I was in the D.A.'s Office by a surprise defense witness.

"Bullshit," Johnny said.
"Come on, Johnny."
"Okay. Okay. Let me get my notes out. All we got is that she spent the night before her murder with her husband, the actor Parker Rinshell, in Sausalito where they have a house."

Parker Rinshell was a distinguished-looking TV and movie actor who mostly did commercials these days. He was quite a few years Amanda's senior and there were persistent rumors about his health. Still they managed to keep one of show business's longest running marriages on the boards.

"And then?" I asked.
"Nothin' else unusual. Not until lunch in the city the next day. That's when she got sick."
"She eat with her husband?"
"No."
"Who'd she eat with?"
"Cleo Maura, it says here. The critic. That's interesting."
That was interesting.
"Where?"
He gave me the name of a Japanese restaurant I knew.
"Probably that sushi shit," he said.
"Hey, not everybody eats Polish kielbasa."
"That's health food compared to raw fish."
"Then what happened?"
"She took a cab back to the theater. She told everybody there she'd be fine by evening. Only she wasn't. She couldn't go on."
"Anybody think to call a doctor?" I asked.

According to St. John

"Sure. But she wouldn't hear of it. Hated doctors like most people hate lawyers. One of those people who can't even look in a medical book."

"And then?" I made the mistake of asking.

"Then Denise Belknap poisoned her. Anything else, St. John? You know I don't got another thing to do but jaw with you all day."

"All I need is Cleo Maura's address and phone number."

"Ever hear of the telephone book?"

"A critic is not going to be listed."

"Yeah. Makes sense."

He came across with Cleo Maura's address and phone number.

I went upstairs and made myself a corned beef, Muenster cheese, and red bell pepper sandwich with hot mustard on a Kaiser roll. I grabbed a kosher dill and a bottle of Henry's and went downstairs. The Chief had gone out to lunch but Mickey had brown bagged it with an unpalatable looking spinach sandwich. We ate on the couch in my office and I told her what I had learned.

"You going to see Cleo Maura?" she asked, taking a bite of my sandwich and a sip of beer.

"Yes. This afternoon."

"Want me along?"

"This is not a paying case. I think you've got to do some tailing of our disability man. The video camcorder's not enough. I'd like to collect our fee on that one."

She agreed. We turned on the answering machine and closed the office down. A month ago that might have meant lovemaking upstairs. Now it meant we were going to work.

Johnny D. had given me a Pacific Heights address which meant Cleo Maura was an affluent as well as influential critic. I took the T-Bird. I expected to find a parking space this time of day in a residential area.

For once I was right. I parked in front of the duplex where she lived. The two-story yellow stucco building was Spanish in design with a large arch over the entrances on each end of the duplex. Palm trees bent over the arches and shaded the thick green plants that almost obscured the walks on each side of the house. Cleo Maura obviously liked her privacy.

I hadn't phoned ahead. I wanted it to be a surprise. Risky but worth it if she was at home. I went through the outer arch on her side of the duplex into a shaded courtyard that you couldn't see from the street. A second interior arch was fitted with a locked ironwork gate. On the wall by the gate was a bell and an intercom.

Cleo Maura was at home. She interviewed me over the intercom, then opened the massive wooden door behind the gate and scrutinized my I.D. through the black bars.

She passed it back through the grill and opened the door with a key. It was the kind of security lock that you had to unlock with a key from both sides.

Close up Cleo Maura looked much as she looked from a distance. Except instead of her trademark floppy hat, her ten-foot orange scarf, and her caftan, she was wearing faded blue jeans and a dirty white sweatshirt that read "Save The Whales." More like a middle-aged housewife than a major San Francisco critic. She was a matronly fortyish. She had a short squat body with a round, cherubic, and not unattractive face. She had eyes the color of root beer candy. Her head was covered with a puffed-up helmet of brown and gray curls. Out of her distinctive costume she didn't look like she had the power to make or break a show.

She led me through one more arch, into a large living room. The interior matched the exterior style. The floor was terra-cotta tile, the walls glazed stone, and the ceiling straw-colored cane. There were dark carpets spread out on the floor and hung up on the walls. Across the room was a large stone fireplace with a mantle that held a Spanish guitar in the center and an unlit candle in a clay holder on each end. Above the room there was a balcony with a wooden railing. Although there was light from the windows that ran along the second story the overwhelming impression of the room was one of dark adobe monotone. I felt as if I were in a Mexican villa or a Mexican restaurant. I wasn't sure which. The only thing missing were pictures of bullfighters on the wall.

"My father left me this duplex when he died. He was a surgeon. This was one of his real estate investments."

"It's . . . nice." Sometimes it's hard to come up with the right word.

We sat down on a distressed wood couch that went with the two circa-1920 Monterey period chairs on the other side of the room. The cushions on each piece were upholstered with an orange and black Aztec pattern. In front of us was a tile and black iron coffee

According to St. John

table that must have weighed two hundred pounds. On it were straw pots and clay vases full of dried flowers.

"Can I get you anything?" she asked.

"No thanks."

She crossed her legs and leaned back. "You wanted to talk about Amanda Cole?"

"Yes." We had gone over all of this during the intercom interview.

"I don't want to help her murderer."

"Neither do I. I want to find out who did it."

"Even if it's Denise Belknap?"

"I can't change the facts. I'm willing to take a chance it won't be Miss Belknap."

"Good luck." Cleo Maura got up. "This is very difficult for me. I'd like a drink."

She went over to a recessed wet bar, discreetly placed under a stone ledge in the corner of the room."

"Want something?"

"Whatever you're having."

"A Margarita."

"Perfect."

She took out a pitcher, poured in prepared Margarita mix and tequila from a Jose Cuervo bottle without measuring. She scooped in shaved ice, stirred, and then reached into a cabinet for two stemmed glasses. She dipped their rims in salt and poured the drinks.

When she put the glasses down on two straw coasters I felt like I should tip her.

"You panned Denise's performance."

She sipped her Margarita. I took a large swallow through the salt.

"I didn't think you were here to discuss the theater."

"I was there opening night."

"And you liked what you saw?" she asked.

I couldn't help grinning. "Yes."

"Prurient interest. Walking around on stage in the nude does not constitute acting."

"But those scenes between her and Atwil before the intermission . . . and the way she played the fourth witch. . ."

She cut me off. "Mr. St. John, if you disagree with my review write a letter to the editor."

"Call me Jeremiah."

"Now, Jeremiah, can we get on with it? I've got some work to get to." She sipped her Margarita.

I wondered who she was going to chew up today. I took another swallow and said, "Okay. I understand you had lunch with Amanda Cole the day she died."

"Yes."

"Isn't that a bit unusual?"

She looked at me curiously. "Very unusual. Most of the people I have lunch with live to tell about it."

Some attempt at black humor. I tried again. "I mean you were going to review her performance that night."

She took a long sip. "We're both professionals."

"But still. . ."

"Still nothing. I don't appreciate your implication. Do you think I could be bought with a lunch? Come on. Besides, I paid. I've got the receipt to prove it."

This wasn't getting me anywhere. "Did you know her long?" I asked.

"Ten years or so. Since she first came to the city."

"Did you see her often?"

"Not very. As you implied, I can't allow myself to get too friendly with any one actor or actress."

"Her getting sick. Was it something she ate?"

"Oh yes. Sushi. She's allergic to raw seafood."

"Oh? So she just ordered some anyway?"

"And she's allergic to alcohol." Cleo finished her drink, picked up mine, and went over to the wet bar. Without asking me she poured out two more drinks.

"That could make life tough. But she drank anyway?"

"Not usually." She was back with the Margaritas. No salt this time.

"Why the odd behavior?" I asked her as she sat back down.

She took a sip of the fresh drink. "She was very upset. When she's like that she denies her allergies. She drinks like a fish to prove she's not allergic to booze. She eats raw seafood for the same damn reason."

"And always ends up sick?"
"As a dog," she said.
"What made her upset?" I asked.
"Are you sure you want to know?"
"I'm sure."
She got out a cigarette from a straw box on the table.
"Care for one?"
"I don't smoke."
"Mind if I do?"
"Speaking of allergies, I'm allergic."
"What kind of P.I. are you?"
"The new breed. Like Spenser."
"At least you drink."
"You bet," I said and swallowed some more of the Margarita. Cleo followed suit. I repeated my question.
"What upset her was the fight she had on Monday with Denise Belknap. She was afraid Denise would do anything to get the part away from her."
"Anything like what?"
"Like balling the director."
"Amanda was the star."
"Stars fade. It's a fact of the theater as well as of the universe."
"And Amanda believed Denny would do anything?" I wanted to pin this down.
"She said that she was afraid of Denise. She was afraid she'd kill for the part."
"Come on."
"Because she would have done it herself when she was young."
Good clean competition. "And you told all of this to the police?"
"Of course."
"Was there much drug use in the company?"
"I wouldn't know anything about that," she said archly, reminding me of another denial I had heard.
"Venture a guess?"
"No."
"What about Amanda herself?"
"Never."
"She was trying to score some coke the night she died."
"I don't know anything about that part of her life. Understand?"

I understood. We were done. I drained my glass and watched her do the same. I thanked her and let her walk me out to the gate. She unlocked it from the inside.

As she swung the gate open I asked, "Do you live here alone?"

"Yes."

I looked back into her villa and nodded.

8

On Friday morning Chief Moses was pursuing the renegade father. Mickey had some good photos of our disability case playing racquetball at his health club. He had been dumb enough to use a court with glass walls. She also had extensive videotape of him walking around without the cane he always used at the insurance office. Apparently it never occurs to these jokers that someone could be watching them. That people, even insurance people, don't like being ripped off.

Since she had it wrapped up, when Scott Forsander called and asked me to come over I invited her along, knowing that would make him happy.

We took the cable car.

Mickey was amused by the decor of Scott Forsander's office. "I especially like the bronze basketball," she said.

"Thanks. It's new." Her sarcasm was lost on him.

Very new. I hadn't seen it there two days ago.

Brian Samaho joined us this morning. Both he and Scott were in three-piece muted plaid suits. Brian, with his hair in a dark brush cut, looked like a teenager dressed up for a field trip to the courthouse.

"I've got the Forensics Report and the final M.E. Autopsy Report," Brian said, indicating the file in his hand.

"Anything new?" I asked as we all sat down. Brian sat on the edge of Scott's desk.

"Not much, but I'll summarize it," he said. He opened up the file then put on horn-rimmed glasses I never saw him wear before.

"When did you get glasses?" I asked.

"I got them to make me look older. They're just plain glass."

It wasn't working but I kept quiet about it.

"I spoke to the medical tech in the Coroner's Office. To get some of the jargon translated into English."

"Just don't turn it into lawyerese," I said.

"Can't understand the mother tongue anymore?" Scott asked.

"I hope not."

Brian looked down at the papers. "Let's do this chronologically. First she got sick at lunch. The Toxicology Report showed toxins in her bloodstream from several allergic reactions. Food and alcohol mainly."

"Then she came back to the theater and tried to score some coke," I said.

"There was a small amount of metabolized cocaine in her brain. And traces of potassium cyanide," Brian said.

"A horrible way to go," Scott said.

"Pathology showed acute inflammation of the right nasal passage. The cyanide hit her so quick she only got one snort. Right to the brain."

"She knew it was bad right away?" I asked.

"She knew this was no ordinary blow. Nausea. Faintness. Falling blood pressure. Convulsions almost immediately. Death."

"You said metabolized cocaine," I said. "That means she used the stuff earlier. How much earlier?"

"Couldn't pin it down. Less than one to more than twenty-four hours."

"That gives us some interesting possibilities." All the more reason to know exactly what Amanda did the day and night before she died.

According to St. John

Brian turned back to his papers. "There were traces of tainted cocaine on Amanda's fingers and on her nostrils. Seems to be no question that the woman snorted the stuff. The chemical tests on the cocaine sample indicated a high quality coke cut with an infant laxative powder—pretty standard operating procedure—and with potassium cyanide—not your usual cutting compound. The coke composition on her fingers and nose matches the cocaine in the room and on Denny's hand mirror in her dressing room."

"That it?" I asked.

"So far for physical evidence."

Unfortunately there was a lot more to go on than just physical evidence.

I looked at the Bay Area through the tenth-floor window. How long before the inevitable high rise would be built to block the view? Probably not until after a court battle with Forsander and Samaho and all the other tenants on that side of the building. That would keep a hell of a lot of lawyers busy, which was exactly what every one of them wanted. What else can you do when the city has nearly 12,000 practicing attorneys, which works out to a ratio of one lawyer for every 62 residents. Only Washington, D.C., is a greater disaster area, with a ratio of 25-1. I was glad to go uncounted as one no longer practicing law. Striking a blow for a lower ratio.

"Who's handling this in the D.A.'s Office?" I asked.

"A deputy D.A. named Howard Vorflagel."

I looked at Mickey.

"We know him," Mickey said.

"He can be very good," Scott said.

"And very bad," Brian added.

"We know. We've seen him in court," I said. "And it looks like it's coming together nicely for him."

"I'm afraid so," Scott said.

"What do you think?" I asked.

"I think we need our defense investigator to come up with something," Brian said as he tapped the edges of the file on the desk.

"By the way," Scott said, "we won our game last night in the City League."

"Without me?" I asked.

"How could that possibly happen?" This time Mickey's sarcasm was not lost on Scott.

Brian moved across the room to the door. "Wish me luck," he said. "I'm going to a bond hearing for Ms. Belknap this morning."

We did.

I didn't want to volunteer Mickey and by extension the St. John Agency, so I asked, somewhat disingenuously, "Even if you get bail set, where will she get the money? You said she was broke."

"First things first," Brian said as he went out.

"Details. Just details," Scott added with a smile. He knew something that he wasn't telling us. That was okay. Sooner or later I would find out.

In the elevator Mickey suggested, "Maybe if we concentrated on where someone could get potassium cyanide."

"That's too wide open at this point. I think we need another approach. One thing is clear. This whole thing was carefully planned. Someone was waiting for an opportunity to put Amanda on ice."

"So we need some motives."

"Besides Denny's."

We left the office building and split up. Mickey was going to the insurance company on Van Ness with the pictures and the tapes of our disability case. Our client was going to love the racquetball sequence.

I walked a block south and a block east to the brokerage house to explain my plan to the president.

The chief executive was a deceptively charming but hard-nosed guy who was in his sixties and looked like he only ate raw fruits and vegetables and ran ten miles every day. He kept his head shaved bald. I suspected he would have very little hair if he let it grow in. Every time I saw him he had on a black suit in a fabric that had raw silk in it and a red tie that was too long for him. He must have thought the extra long tie gave him a power look.

He listened. He liked it. He set up an account for me with a credit line to deal in futures.

"Just don't lose too much money," he said.

"It'll be a good investment," I told him.

"I still can't believe it could be Carrie."

"I'm betting on it."

"I almost hope you're wrong," he said.

"This is our best lead."

"If it's her, get the bitch."

According to St. John

"That's more like it."

He called our stockbroker suspect and told her he had a new client for her.

"Won't she be suspicious?" I asked.

"No. This is standard procedure. I'll talk to a client and then refer them to an account exec."

The question was how long would it take for her to trust me enough to try to get me involved in the scam.

I went out to Carrie's desk in the center of the large open office and introduced myself.

Carrie was an attractive woman in her late twenties. She was wearing a dark business suit with a light blue blouse and a red scarf knotted like a tie. Her blond hair was pulled back in a bun. Behind mannish black-rimmed glasses she had light blue eyes. She was very carefully made up. She was probably one of those women who took more than a half-hour to put on her face in the morning.

When we got to talking I was impressed with what she seemed to know about the market.

She put me into some futures and promised to monitor the account daily.

We shook hands on it.

"Could I use your phone?" I asked. "A local call."

"Of course." She was polite enough to walk away from her desk to give me a little privacy. But not much since there was another broker at the next desk. At least he was busy making a sales pitch on the phone for some obscure over-the-counter stocks.

I wasn't sure where the odds were better. Nevada or the market. The only thing I knew was that the house always took its cut first. Both gambling house and brokerage house.

I used her phone to check in with Forsander.

"Come on back here. Denny's out."

9

"I convinced Her Honor that Denny wasn't going to skip out. Not with the part of Lady Macbeth to play," Brian said.

Scott, Brian, and I were sitting with Denny in a small conference room between the partners' private offices. It had the same great view of the bay. The only thing better was the view of Denny sitting at the table in front of the window. Her brief jail stay hadn't affected her much. She turned to look at the bay. I looked at her profile.

There were no ashtrays on the oak table or anywhere else in the room. Here Forsander and Samaho had the same No Smoking sign I had in my office. Here there were no signs of Scott's basketball days. Just several large abstract oil paintings done by the same artist. The way he splattered his colors—reds, greens, oranges, golds—they all looked like variations on a sunburst colliding with a tornado.

"So we got bail set at $250,000," Brian said.

"Good work. That left $25,000 to come up with for the bail bondsman," I noted. The going rate was ten percent if you could find someone to handle such a large bail.

No one seemed concerned about the source of this money. I wasn't going to say a word about Mickey and the agency. Twenty-five grand was out of our league.

Denny turned back to me. "The theater company put it up."

So that was what Scott was holding back from me. Denny did have money behind her. That sonofabitch.

As for the theater company, it wasn't a bad investment. With Denny in jail the run of *Macbeth* had to be suspended. But with her out and acting in the play, considering the incredible free publicity in the press—including shadowed photos of the sleepwalk—the potential for ticket sales was staggering.

"Have any questions?" Scott asked me.

"I do. About our financial arrangement. But we can discuss that later." If the theater company was springing for twenty-five grand they had to be coming up with legal fees as well. Which meant the agency could be paid. But with Denny here I would just play the defense investigator.

"I meant for Denny."

"I know." I turned to her. "Let's nail this down," I said. "Several witnesses saw you leave Amanda's room right before the play began. Then no one sees her until the director finds the body."

"I guess," she said.

"Could the tainted cocaine have been there already?"

"I don't see why not. I didn't bring it."

"But she had tried to score some coke just before you went in to see her."

"Well, she didn't get any from me," Denny said.

"No. But the traces of coke in your dressing room contained the cyanide," I said.

"I didn't have any coke in my dressing room!"

"How did it get there?" I asked.

"The damn door was never locked. Anybody could have brought it in."

"She has a point," Scott said.

"And where would I get this cyanide shit?"

84

According to St. John

"That's not a concern of the police right now. What they care about are traces of the murder powder on your hand mirror."

She reached for her purse. "Do you mind if I smoke?"

Brian and Scott pointed out the sign to her.

"Christ," she muttered.

"Secondary smoke is worse than primary. It leads to shortened breath which leads to not being able to make it down a basketball court on a fast break," Brian said.

"That really breaks my heart," she said, but she didn't pull out her cigarettes. "At least in jail I could smoke."

"I've got to ask you the tough one, Denny," I said.

"No problem. I didn't kill her."

"That's not the question I meant. How much are you into cocaine? Do you have a habit?"

Denny turned to face me squarely. "And someone with a habit would kill to get the kind of job that would pay the money to feed it? Well I'm not into cocaine. I'll take a blow on the weekend. Or at a party if it's around."

"Just being sociable?" I asked.

"Yes!" she said angrily. "Like a lot of others in the cast and crew. We're no better or worse than anyone else in society."

"But you did buy cocaine Sunday night?" I asked.

"A Candy Man was around and I bought."

I didn't mention that she had lied to me.

"Did you use any?"

"Some. What was left I flushed down the toilet Wednesday morning."

"That's too bad. Now there's no chance to compare samples."

"I was afraid the cops would search my place and bust me for possession."

"Better than murder," Brian threw in.

"A dilemma," I said.

"Look," Denny insisted. "I don't do drugs. I mean I hardly ever do drugs. I'm not an addict."

"Did you ever smoke crack?" I asked.

"No!"

I didn't think she was a coke head but I was on her side. How would a jury react to her?

"Could anyone have gone back to Amanda's dressing room once the play began?" I asked.

"I hope so," Denny said. She rubbed her fingers together nervously.

I looked at Scott and Brian. They seemed content to leave the questioning to me.

"Who?" I asked.

"You're the detective," she said.

"Someone else had to have what you had. Means. Motive. Opportunity." I tapped the last three words out on the table with my forefinger. "Let's start with motive."

"I was new in the company. I didn't get much gossip about rivalries."

"Nothing?"

"Well a lot of people didn't like her. Everyone knows that. But nothing specific. Nothing to kill over."

"No conflicts?"

"Nothing out in the open except the one between Amanda and me."

Brian shook his head but said nothing.

"What about opportunity?" I asked.

"Once the production starts it's hard to be alone backstage. And the techs don't leave their stations."

"Maydik found the body. He left."

"Perry's the director. And he was only gone for maybe a couple of minutes."

"It's an impossible window of time, Jeremiah," Brian said.

"It's something," I said.

"You're going to have to do better," Scott said.

"I know."

The partners waited.

"Denny," I persisted, "I saw the dressing room setup. They're all along a corridor in the rear of the building, separated from the working backstage area. To get to them you go down a single hallway then turn right. Is that the only way to get between the private dressing rooms and the backstage area?"

"Yes," Denny said. She was fumbling in her purse. She had to be thinking nicotine fix.

"Could someone have gone back there without being seen by anyone in the backstage area?" I asked.

According to St. John

"Probably," she said.

"Is there a guard back there? Someone to keep away stage door Johnnies?" I asked.

"Stage door Johnnies? How quaint." She laughed. "There are three ways to get backstage. One from outside and two from inside the theater. There's a stage door that opens out on the parking lot. Or you can go right up the steps on the side of the stage. And there's a door to the right of the stage inside the theater off the lobby. The door from the lobby is right by the stage door to the parking lot. For those two doors we have a guard—of sorts."

"Where's this inside door? Stage right?" I asked.

"Yes. Next to the restrooms."

"And there's a guard there?"

"There's supposed to be. Leroy. He even has a uniform."

"Leroy who?" I asked.

"Leroy Washington. He's an old black man with a drinking problem. I think he's Perry's great uncle or something. That's why he keeps him on. During the afternoon he lets the actors in through the stage door. But Leroy is out of it by seven o'clock most nights. Then he goes backstage into the custodian's closet where there's a pillow, a blanket, and a small black-and-white TV."

"So everyone comes in through this stage door?"

"Yeah," Denny said wearily. "I guess so."

"What about other outside doors?" Brian asked.

"There are fire doors we use for exits. They're supposed to be locked from the outside."

Brian turned to me. "A possibility."

"A means. But we've got to concentrate on finding somebody with a motive and opportunity to murder Amanda Cole."

"That's your job," Scott said.

"And Homicide's. But they think they've already done it."

"You're making progress, Jeremiah," Scott said as he stood up and shot his Rolex out from under his cuff. "I've got to run. I'm due in court. You can continue on without me."

"Thanks," I said as he left.

Denny rubbed the bridge of her nose. "I just remembered something," she said.

"What?"

"Amanda Cole used to come in through the fire door by her dressing room."

"How?"

"I guess she had a key."

"Did anyone else?"

"Not that I know of."

"A star's privilege," Brian said.

"That's something to find out about," I said.

Denny leaned forward and put her head in her hands. "I need a break," she said. "I haven't eaten yet."

"Well Brian, shall we take the lady to lunch?"

Brian checked his Rolex. "I had lunch and I have an appointment."

"Then how about the two of us getting something to eat?" I asked her.

"Sure. First I need to powder my nose."

While I waited for Denny I tried to make something of the new information. Nothing specific came of it but it was a way to pass the time until my lunch date returned. Which was not soon. Denny was in the office ladies' room long enough to powder her entire body several times over. Still it was worth it. When she came out there was a fresh blush to her cheeks and a shine to her hair. She'd used perfume but it didn't mask the smell of cigarette smoke. I decided not to let it bother me.

We walked over to my old standby, Monday's.

It was an old-fashioned tavern with comfortable leather-upholstered booths, wood paneling, and wide-bladed ceiling fans. The food was eclectic and decent. The chef was a very creative Hungarian refugee who cooked what he liked to eat.

Since it was close to the courthouse, Monday's was a hangout for attorneys, clerks, legal secretaries, and even judges. And an occasional P.I. or two. It was always interesting to see who was eating with whom. You could speculate on what these meetings meant for cases coming to trial. It was a good place to spot an out-of-court settlement in the making.

By the time we got there the place was nearly deserted. It was long past the noon hour and the lunch crowd had returned to the business of the courts.

We had our choice of booths and in deference to Denny we took one in the smoking section. I must be getting soft, I thought.

According to St. John

As I slid in across from Denny I gave a wave of recognition to the bartender, Nelson Bittenbender. He was tall, well-muscled without being overly developed, handsome in a pouting, long-faced way, and very gay. He sported an 1890's waxed handlebar mustache which looked good on him. In the past he had been a somewhat reluctant informant for me.

Nelson nodded in response.

A waitress with two-tone hair made her way over to us. Denny ordered a double Smirnoff martini on the rocks with a twist. She had a few bad days to shake off. I settled for a Henry's.

We made small talk, avoiding the case for now, until the waitress finally appeared with our drinks. I wondered how long she took when there were other customers in the place. Denny ordered a shrimp salad and a second double. I went for a medium rare burger with french fries, half of an onion log, and another beer.

Denny was relaxing. She had even forgotten about her cigarettes. She started talking about her career and her dreams. The murder of Amanda Cole was nothing more than a newspaper story. For the moment.

When the food came Denny went at it ravenously, eating everything including the two cups of cocktail sauce.

"I'm still hungry." She took a french fry from my plate.

I signaled the waitress. Denny ordered a hamburger with everything.

"I'm going to start talking to the cast and crew," I said. I had wanted to start with Maydik. The police had interviewed him but Johnny D. had not passed anything on. So far the man had dropped out of sight. At least for me. Leroy was obvious too. "Got any suggestions on where to start besides Maydik and Leroy? I'd like someone who's been around a while. Preferably a drinker who likes to talk." I handed her one of my remaining two fries.

"I'm not sure, Jeremiah."

"Take a stab at it."

She took a stab with the fry into the pool of ketchup on my plate. "Eric Ullwanger," she said. "He plays Donalbain. I've seen him smashed enough times."

"Talkative?"

"Very."

89

"It's a start."

I looked for our waitress but there was no sign of her or Denny's order. I dipped my last fry in ketchup and held it up to her. She leaned over and bit it, nicking my fingers with her teeth. Then she said, "I appreciate everything you're doing."

"All I'm doing is feeding you french fries."

"I'm serious."

"Anything for a friend of my partner. Especially when she's so beautiful."

She reached out and took my hand. Her fingers were cold from the martini glass. I wondered about Amanda's charge that Denny had been sleeping with the director. How does an understudy end up with a private dressing room next to the star's?

When Denny's hamburger platter arrived, I ordered a third Henry's, and tried to forget that she had lied to me about the cocaine.

The waitress was looking expectantly at Denny.

"I'll pass on the drinks," she said then smiled at me. "I don't want to make the same list as Eric."

Mickey was back at the office alone. She had closed her case except for her testimony at a disability review board hearing. She was ready for a new assignment.

I went into my office and Mickey followed. She flopped back on my couch.

"What's next?" she asked.

"Nothing new right now," I said. "But we could try something a little old."

Mickey looked at me with annoyance. "Jeremiah, there's nothing more between us. What we had was . . . a brief sexual encounter . . . an indiscretion. I wish you'd forget about it."

I laughed. "I can't."

"Try."

"I don't want to, Mickey."

"Try anyway. And please burn that damn picture of me."

"Never. You know how hard it was to find?"

"We should never have gone to bed together."

"Why not?"

"Not while we're working together."

According to St. John

"Why not? We're equals. We're partners."

"It's not professional."

We'd had this discussion too many times already. It always ended up the same way. Still, I couldn't help trying to make her jealous.

"Then you don't mind if I ask Denny out?"

Mickey sat up stiffly. Her face flushed down to her throat. "No. Why should I?" She got up. "I've still got some typing to do on that damn antique." She went back to her desk. The reaction I wanted. More or less.

"Maybe I will," I said softly. I went straight to the phone to call Scott Forsander and said, "The situation has changed. The Marina Theater Company has the money and I assume they're paying your bills. Which means we reopen negotiations."

"Which means?"

"That the agency expects to get paid."

"You took this on spec for future work, Jeremiah," Scott said, but I could hear in his voice that he was wavering. I hoped he was feeling guilty about our deal.

"Bullshit! That's when there was no money."

There was a long silence on the line.

"At least let me hear the Beach Boy tape," I said.

"Okay, St. John. What are you asking for?"

I told him our usual terms.

He countered. We compromised. Lower terms for future work. I was pleased. Basketball networking again.

"Can I change the subject?" Scott asked.

"Sure." I had my feet up on the desk. I was feeling like a winner. If I smoked I would have lit up a cigar.

"How's the back?"

"Improving." I said. "What's that got to do with anything?"

"I just got another call. We lost another player."

"That's what happens in the Over-30 league. Don't count on me for this season."

"I'm getting desperate."

"Get your mind occupied with something else. How about the Denise Belknap case for example?"

I hung up and gave serious consideration to the idea of calling up Denny.

As I picked up the phone, I heard the Chief come in after a day of tracking the missing Slater and son through the wilds of the city. I put the phone down.

I called Mickey and the Chief into my office. "Good news," I told them, "We are now on the Forsander and Samaho payroll and future business will be directed to us as well."

"It's not a bleeding heart charity case?" the Chief asked.

"No more."

"We will save this squaw."

"Which one? Denny or Mickey?"

"Both, Jeremiah. Both," the Chief concluded.

10

That Friday evening we heard from the perky black-haired co-anchor of one of the local news shows that *Macbeth* was going to reopen Sunday and that a rehearsal was already scheduled for tonight. Her comments were more or less objective.

Then came the editorial from the news director. He denounced Denny's release on bail and the quick reopening of the play with Denny as Lady Macbeth. He termed it "commercial crassness at its worst." Then he mentioned the threats made by some organizations to picket or otherwise disrupt the performance. The groups ranged from anti-pornography to TOC—Tough on Crime—which saw Denny's release as another example of a fish-belly-soft judiciary. He called for peaceful demonstrations and the immediate reclosing of the play. Good luck.

"Divergent views expressed by responsible spokespersons are welcome to free air time for rebuttal."

"Want to go on? Either of you?" I asked my partners.

Mickey shut off the portable color TV I kept in the back of a closet. I rolled it away.

"I think we should visit this rehearsal," I said. I was hoping to get a chance to talk to Perry Maydik.

The Chief said he had some private business to attend to. When he said "private business" it was better not to ask any questions. Besides you could never get an answer.

So the Chief went his own way while Mickey and I went to the theater. Given the media exposure I was surprised to find only a couple of pickets out in front protesting the reopening of the play on various moral grounds. There was a van from the same local TV station we had watched taping and interviewing the two of them. Pretty meager for a news event. The big test would be when the show reopened Sunday afternoon.

We showed our I.D.'s through the glass doors to a young Hispanic woman who was vacuuming the lobby, and asked to be let in. She shook her head and indicated that she didn't understand. With that she promptly disappeared. A few minutes later she came back with one of the women who worked in the box office. This person scrutinized our I.D.'s and finally unlocked a door. Great cooperation so far.

I went in search of Maydik and was told that he wasn't coming in tonight, that he was up at his Tahoe home, and that his assistant was handling this rehearsal. If he turned out to be hard to find, I might have to send the Chief to track him down.

Leroy wasn't around either tonight. I would give Maydik's assistant a try.

She was a tall black woman who wore large hoop earrings that dangled to her shoulders. She had on a dark outfit that was cut like a man's suit. With it she wore a wide collared shirt, a knit tie, and black leather boots. Her head was partially shaved so that her scalp showed through. She was standing in the third row taking notes as the witches went through one of their routines. From the intense look on her face I knew this was no time to bother her with questions about Amanda Cole's murder. Or anything else.

Mickey and I sat down a few rows behind her.

During the break I approached Maydik's assistant, but she was involved in a frantic conversation with the actress playing Lady Macduff. She motioned me away with a wave of her hand. She had

According to St. John

the longest nails I had ever seen on a woman. I retreated for the moment. Mickey caught up with Denny and asked her to set it up with Ullwanger for us since Maydik and even Leroy were unavailable. She agreed to give it a try.

I decided to tour the building. I went to the rear of the theater and up into the balcony. I went back downstairs and followed a sign that pointed to steps to my left. They led up to the private box area, where I pulled aside a curtain and looked into one of the boxes. Good view of the rehearsal that was underway again. I went down a second flight of stairs that brought me to the front of the theater by the restrooms and the doors to backstage and the parking lot that Denny had mentioned. No one was guarding them right now. I had a much better idea of how the foot traffic flowed through the theater.

I took a seat next to Mickey just in time to see Eric Ullwanger as the lame and bitter Donalbain return to Scotland. I hadn't paid much attention to the actor before but this time I concentrated on him.

He was tall and thin, with a bush of black hair so high it looked like an electrified wig. It easily added three inches to his height. I guessed he was in his late twenties.

While on stage they were announcing Lady Macbeth's suicide, Denny came out in her costume to see us. She looked exhausted. All she said was "Eric will meet you in the lobby when he's finished. But I've got to warn you. He's acting strange tonight." She hurried away before I could ask her to explain.

When the rehearsal ended I tried to talk to the assistant director again but she brushed me off and went backstage. So Mickey and I walked out into the empty lobby to wait. Twenty minutes later Ullwanger showed up in jeans and a white fisherman's sweater. The freaky hair was his. My guess on his age had been off. Without makeup his skin was mottled and had enough lines to put him in his late thirties.

He looked at us with dark brown eyes that were bloodshot. Then he started to back away. He looked very unhappy. He acted strange, like he was having second thoughts about talking to us. We didn't want him changing his mind, so Mickey and I moved swiftly.

Before Ullwanger could retreat any further Mickey introduced us and thanked him for agreeing to talk to us. She even took his arm. She wasn't going to lose this one.

"I'm not sure I'm up to this," he said.

"Let's go someplace comfortable," I suggested. "How about the Marina Green Yacht Club bar? I'm buying." Ullwanger brightened just enough.

The Marina Green Yacht Club was close to the theater, close enough to walk to. The three of us went out into the cold October night. The sky was thick with bright clusters of stars. The Golden Gate Bridge was to the west, its twin towers rising in spotlights. Only the shadow of Alcatraz loomed ominous in the moonlight.

To keep warm we walked quickly.

At the ornately carved doors of the yacht club I showed a membership card that was part of my collection of useful business and membership cards that I had managed to gather. One of my favorite ways is to go up to a bulletin board in a bar covered with business cards and stick up mine while removing three or four other ones I could use. Memberships are a little more difficult but enough have managed to come my way. This card was good enough to get us past the doorman who was dressed in a blue sea captain's uniform complete with hat and boots. The outfit made him look like something from an ad for frozen fish sticks. I had the feeling the doorman didn't much care for the costume and didn't much care who got by him. I scrawled something illegible in the member's sign-in book and the three of us swept into the bar.

It was as self-consciously nautical as the doorman. The walls were covered with framed pictures of every kind of ship I could think of and a few more, from Yankee Clippers to Mississippi River boats to oil tankers. The plank floor looked like the deck of a sailing ship and there was a ship's wheel at the far end of the room for anyone who wanted to do a little steering. It looked like a spot for a photo opportunity. The bar itself gleamed with varnish. The miniature brass ship's wheels along the face of the bar counter looked newly polished. Behind the bar were two men in plain red jackets. I wondered if their union contract protected them from wearing costumes.

We took a round wooden table by the glass wall that looked out over the moored boats of the yacht club. The chairs were the kind you always find in seafood restaurants: wooden and hard with un-

According to St. John

comfortable bars in the curved back. The place wasn't crowded so we would have plenty of privacy.

We ordered drinks from a lemon-haired waitress who was wearing a navy blue, red, and white sailor suit—the kind you see on kids. Only this one had a mini skirt and was worn with black textured stockings and black spike heels.

Mickey asked about the house white and ordered a half carafe.

Eric surprised me when he asked about beers on tap. He ended up ordering a large pitcher of Moosehead. I was tempted but I went with the usual, a bottle of Henry's. Eric looked relieved that he didn't have to share.

The pitcher made it easy for Eric to consume the beer without having to get the waitress back. Only the beer tends to get flat if it sits in the pitcher too long. Usually with one person that's a problem. But not for Eric.

We spent most of the first pitcher on Amanda Cole and her relationship to other members of the company.

"She was a bitch," Eric said to sum it up. Then he rattled off a list of names. "They all hated her."

It was long and impressive. Mickey jotted the names down in shorthand.

The assistant director whose name was Leah X. was on it.

"X?" I asked. "A follower of Muhammad X. and Malcolm?"

"A recent convert. X'ed out her slave name which happened to be Grant. Hates whites in general. Amanda in particular."

I ordered Eric a second pitcher which would have to carry him through the night. I had another Henry's. Mickey was still working her way through the house white.

"Which one could have killed Amanda Cole?" Mickey asked as she looked at her list of names.

Eric put a thoughtful look on his face then poured himself a fresh mug of Moosehead. The first glass came out about half foam but it didn't seem to bother him.

"Any of them," he said. There was a foam mustache over his lip. He looked like a wild-haired kid—with a ruddy mottled face and large very sad eyes. Something was depressing the man. I hoped it wasn't us.

My second Henry's was gone. I held up the bottle to order another.

Eric ran his fingers through his mound of hair like a rake. If it had been a toupee he would have pulled it off with the force he used.

I was getting impatient. I was about to prod him again when he suddenly slammed his empty mug down and announced, "Perry Maydik."

The guy had brought us around to the man who found the body. Brilliant.

"Why?" Mickey pursued.

"Artistic differences."

Bullshit I thought.

"Such as?" she asked.

"Amanda wouldn't do the nude scene," he explained.

"Too modest?" I asked. I doubted it.

"Actually, she said it was like defacing a monument. Doing what Perry wanted to do to Shakespeare." he laughed grimly. "But I think it was because she was too old and saggy in the wrong places. Nobody in this business is modest. You can't afford it." He waved his wrist in a mannered gesture of dismissal. "You should have seen what I had to do when I died as Edward II in Marlowe's play." His voice had gone to a higher pitch that seemed close to hysteria.

I knew the play and didn't want to hear from an hysterical actor about how a red hot iron poker enema was staged. So I quickly asked, "What else do you have?"

It took a moment for Eric to compose himself.

"God. The whole concept. Perry demanded real sexual tension. He wanted Macbeth to be obsessed with his wife. And driven to his acts by the fear that she would kick him out of her bed if he didn't make her queen. Amanda took a different approach. Lady Macbeth as tormented victim of the male's bloody ambition."

"Couldn't Maydik just dump her?"

"Amanda Cole? No way. She had an ironclad contract. He would have to go before she did. That's why she did whatever the hell she wanted."

"Who wrote that contract for her?" Mickey asked. "Not Maydik?"

"The producer. Julian Kismodel."

"What do you know about him?" I asked.

According to St. John

"Nothing. He's like the phantom of the opera. You almost never see him. He just pays the bills."

A possibility. Kismodel and Amanda Cole.

"Was there anything personal?" I asked.

"What do you mean?" Eric asked.

"Anything between the producer and Amanda?"

"We never see him. I told you."

"Not even the star?" Mickey asked.

"You're asking the wrong guy."

I tried something else. "Anything between Amanda and Maydik?"

"No."

The waitress in the sexy sailor suit passed by to check if we needed anything.

"A motive," I said.

Her face scrunched up in thought. "Is that some kinda drink?" she asked.

"We're fine," I said to her. I turned back to Eric. "Was Amanda Cole screwing around with anybody?"

"She didn't run around on her husband."

"Are you sure?"

"You would hear things if something was going on."

"Maybe," I said.

"For sure. This is a very incestuous group," Eric said. The words were beginning to slur. Eric dropped his head lower to his mug. It was like the two pitchers hit him all at once. I suspected these were not his first drinks of the day. When he looked up he said, "Somebody else been snoopin' around. He asked me some questions the other night." His concentration and words were fuzzy.

"The cops are investigating a murder," I said. "They talk to people. It's their job."

"No. This guy was some kinda private dick, like you."

Eric now had the brain of a Moosehead and was about as articulate.

"What was this guy's name?" Mickey asked.

We waited. I began to wonder if Eric had heard the question. Or maybe he had forgotten what she asked.

"I don't remember, he finally said. "But I got his card." He took out his wallet and started going through its contents. It took about five minutes for Eric to realize that he didn't have this mysterious P.I.'s card.

So he would know who to call in case he remembered anything else I tucked one of our agency cards into his wallet.

Who the hell besides us was working on this case?

"Where'd he take you?" I asked. I figured this P.I. had done his homework too. He had Eric pegged as a drinker and talker.

"The Buena Vista."

A crowded tourist place at the end of a cable car run near Ghirardelli Square and the Cannery. Its claim to fame was that it was where Irish Coffee was introduced to the American drinker.

I tried to get him to talk about the Candy Man who had been supplying the company but Eric was hopeless.

I paid the bill in cash since my credit card didn't match the name on my membership card. Eric disappeared into the men's room and Mickey and I waited in the lobby. More pictures of boats. Large framed plans of ten-meter racing yachts. A wooden chandelier in the shape of a ship's wheel over our heads. A fireplace in the shape of the bow of a ship.

"Thematic decorating," I said.

"Is he ever coming out?"

"A couple pitchers of Moosehead will do that to you," I said and went in to get him. I had to help him through the men's room door and the lobby.

I felt guilty about abandoning Eric in his beered-out state so I piled him into the T-Bird with an unhappily crushed Mickey. We managed to get an address that we could understand after several attempts at it.

It was a short ride. The apartment was above a bar on Bay Street not far from Fisherman's Wharf. The perfect habitat for Eric Ullwanger. By the time we got there Eric was snoring. When we woke him up he started to cry.

He needed help going up the steps and Mickey and I each took an arm. We got the door unlocked for him and nudged him in. That was it. No undressing. No wiping away the tears. No tucking in bed. From then on he was on his own.

"Life ain't fuckin' fair," he shouted as I closed the door. No shit.

"A very sad man," I said.

Mickey nodded. "For a lot of reasons."

"Some worth finding out." Ullwanger turned out to be more interesting than I expected.

As I drove Mickey back to her Embarcadero apartment I thought I would give it one more try.

"Let's do lunch sometime," I said vaguely.

"Sure," she said equally vaguely.

"Tomorrow?"

"Seriously?"

"Meet me at the office at noon," I said.

"She jerked her head towards me. "Can't you pick me up?"

I kept my eyes on the dark street. "No. Chief promised to tune the T-Bird up tomorrow," I lied. But for a good reason. I was going to cook Mickey a spectacular lunch.

"Some date," she muttered.

I took that for a yes.

11

I got up early Saturday morning and went to the grocery store on Sutter owned and operated by three Vietnamese brothers named Chew who had been part of the boat people flotilla. It was the kind of store that had a green canvas awning that the brothers cranked down by hand each morning. Under its shade they lined up open crates of fresh fruits and vegetables and hung up an outdoor scale next to a box of brown paper bags. With that preparation completed each brother took a different counter and the store was open for business.

In the window was a large bin of ice on which rested a dozen as yet uncleaned fish. As fish go, they were the ugliest I had ever seen. The sign stuck in the ice read "Monk Fish—taste like lobster." Some other day.

I picked up yeast, flour, olive oil, chives, sour cream, and a small jar of black caviar. The Vietnamese brother behind the deli counter was named Chin but he called himself Hank after Henry Aaron for some reason I couldn't fathom but still thought I understood. For that same reason his brothers called themselves Willie and Reggie. During the season the ghetto blaster in the back of the store was constantly tuned to either a Giant or an A's game. This morning it was a countdown of the week's top hits hosted by the immortal Dick Clark.

Hank sliced six ounces of smoked salmon for me, paper thin as I requested. Then he pitched the monk fish which I declined.

"You be sorry," he said as he shook his head.

"Probably."

I picked up my bag of groceries and headed back to my flat.

It was nine o'clock when I got started. I had done this only once before and it had taken three hours. I would just make it if everything went right again.

I dissolved the yeast in a cup of warm water then mixed up the flour, salt, and olive oil to which I added the yeast and water. I kneaded the stuff until it was like a ball of rubber. Then I put it into a bowl and covered it up with a towel to let the dough rise.

I worked out in my gym which probably wasn't good for the dough but I wasn't going to sit there watching it rise for an hour and a half. Even a P.I. used to watching and waiting has to draw the line somewhere. I concluded my workout with twenty minutes on the exercise bicycle and ten minutes in the shower. By then I was ready to take on the damn dough.

I pulled off its towel and popped it out on the table. I proceeded to punch it into submission before sending it to rise for thirty minutes. If nothing else I can read recipes.

I finished dressing and got ready for the penultimate phase. I flattened out the ball of dough with the palms of my hands and then I rolled and stretched it into a circle about a quarter of an inch thick. Nice free form I thought.

I had a half-hour left before Mickey was due. I turned on the old oven to 500 degrees and got to work. I minced the chives and kneaded them into the flattened circle of dough. I got the other ingredients ready then put the dough on the slab of a heavy metal baking sheet.

The crust was ready just before noon. I slid it out of the oven and spread sour cream over it. Then I arranged the slices of salmon on it. The black caviar went in the center, a dark hub that looked like a fish eye. I opened a chilled bottle of Sonoma Gewurztraminer.

According to St. John

As if on cue I heard Mickey unlock the front door.

"I'm here, Jeremiah," she shouted, "just as I promised. And I'm hungry. I haven't eaten all morning."

"Come on up." I slipped the crust and the topping under a foil cover on the counter.

She came up the stairs and I came out on the landing. She looked sexy in a red sweater and gray mini. The skirt was much shorter than anything she would wear to work where she considered exposing too much thigh to be unbusinesslike.

"I've got something to show you," I said.

"I've seen it. It's nothing to write home to mother about."

"That's not what I mean." I was glad we were flirting again.

I waited for the smells from the kitchen to hit her.

She sniffed. "What's that?"

That's what I mean. Lunch."

"I thought we were going out. I dressed to go out."

"I cooked."

"Jesus, Jeremiah." But she didn't look or sound angry. "What do I smell?" She considered. "You actually cooked? You hate to cook."

"I did it for you and I did it from scratch."

"So what is it?"

"Is it driving you crazy with hunger?"

"Yes."

"Then come on in."

I led her to the kitchen counter and unveiled my masterpiece. Mickey looked at it skeptically. "What is it? A Jewish pizza?"

My creation did resemble an oversized bagel covered with sour cream and lox—even to the hole created by the circle of black caviar.

"Actually it's Spago's Smoked-Salmon-and-Caviar Pizza after the recipe of Chef Wolfgang Puck of Spago in L.A."

Mickey picked up the bottle of wine and read the label.

"Still want to go out?"

"My favorite wine, too."

"Is that all you've got to say?"

She pulled up a formica chair to the formica table and sat down. I put the pizza in the center of it.

"Stop asking questions and slice it before it gets cold."

"The way to a woman's heart . . ."

"If you talk nonsense I'm leaving."

I shut up and sliced the pizza with a roller cutter just like a pro. Mickey poured the wine.

Mickey took a bite and said, "Wonderful."

We ate all that we could handle and still had a third of a pizza left. I refilled our wine glasses.

I stared at Mickey's face until our eyes made contact and held. I was ready to go beyond flirting.

"We can play it straight. No sex in the office. No sex on stakeouts. No sex in the T-Bird. No sex until after five except on the weekends and holidays . . ."

"Don't spoil it, Jeremiah."

I reached out over the Spago pizza to take her hand and said, "Move in with me."

This drove her to drink. She swallowed down the rest of her glass of wine and poured herself another.

I got up and walked around behind her. "Can't we just start over? Get it right this time?"

"Oh Jeremiah," she said as she turned around and took both of my hands in hers. Maybe I was getting it right.

"Move in with me. You wouldn't have to ride the cable car every morning. You could sleep late and still get to work on time."

She dropped my hands and spun back around. "I'm not ready for that kind of commitment."

"So much for the aphrodisiac powers of Spago pizza. Maybe if I had used the golden caviar . . ."

Mickey smiled and I laughed. It was the best we could do considering.

We heard the Chief's heavy unmistakeable footsteps downstairs. It was unusual for him to show up on Saturday.

We went down and into his office. He was sitting at his desk studying some hand-drawn plans.

He looked at us with solemn dark eyes but didn't say a thing about the private business he had gone on last night.

"What are you doing, Chief?" I asked.

"Working."

"On the runaway husband?" It didn't seem like it to me.

"That one will take a little time for the Great Tracker. I went over what little Mrs. Slater had. The woman he had been seeing in the city before he disappeared could be a lead. I will make some phone calls on Monday."

"And then some traveling?" I asked.

"When I know where to go." Then the Great Tracker sniffed the air. "What is that?"

"We left some pizza upstairs. Want some?" I asked.

"What kind?"

"Picky," Mickey said.

"Salmon and caviar on sour cream a la Spago."

He smiled. "I prefer the Chez Panisse pizza with Gorgonzola and Rosemary."

"No shit," I said.

"I had lunch at Chew's grocery."

"What's this?" Mickey asked as she picked up the diagram on his desk.

"I stopped at the Marina Theater to get a set of floor plans. The best the house manager could do was a seating plan. No one knew what had happened to the architect's plans so I made my own sketch."

"Nice job," I said as we gathered around his desk.

"A talent of my people. From sand painting."

"Those are the Navajos."

"Up yours, pale face."

"Peace," I said.

"With honor only."

"Whatever."

We went over the plans in detail. Unlike my brief tour yesterday the Chief had gone into the two distinct backstage areas. The first was directly behind the stage and contained the tech areas, the prop shop, and the director's office. This was also the area from which the actors would enter on stage. The actors and the crew had all been back there. A lot of alibis for the company.

The other backstage area was to stage right of the prop shop and the main stage. Here the actors would dress and get made up as they prepared to go on. You could reach this area by coming off the stage or passing Leroy's checkpoint. The basic pattern of the area consisted of two parallel halls and a third one perpendicular to these. The Chief had marked them Corridors A B C—with C perpendicular to A and B. If you came from the stage you would have to pass through the makeup room to get to Corridor A. To go to Corridor B and Amanda Cole's dressing room you would have to go along A, past costume storage, a fitting room, the costume shop, the laundry and dye room, and more storage. You then took a quick right at the end of A on what the Chief had marked Corridor C to get to the private dressing rooms where Amanda Cole was murdered. I traced the path to B with my finger.

"Convoluted," Mickey said.

"But not impossible," I said.

"With a high probability of being seen," Chief Moses added.

Then he traced the straight line of Corridor C as it ran from Leroy back to Corridor B and the dressing rooms.

"Neat and elegant."

"Once you get past Leroy."

"What about all of these fire doors?" Mickey asked. As in any public building the fire exits were numerous.

"Locked from the outside."

"But one could have been opened," I said. "I'd like to take another look at this setup in person."

"First," the Chief said, "I will finish the Spago pizza." We marched upstairs.

I called ahead and spoke to Jose Zambrini, the house manager. He was in the lobby waiting for us when we arrived. He was a dark short man with thinning hair and a scraggly goatee. The plaid shirt he wore was struggling to come out of the waistband of his pants. The slacks themselves were hoisted over his gut by a pair of suspenders. He let us in but he didn't look happy. He looked worried.

He had let the Chief in earlier in the day. Now the Chief was back with us. Nevertheless he put on the house lights for us in the empty theater.

We went directly to the entrance to Corridor C and the door to the parking lot which Leroy would have been guarding. I sat down on the stool that Leroy would sit on until he disappeared into the broom closet.

To my right were restrooms for the audience. To my left, across a small lobby, were the double doors that an usher would be stationed at during a performance.

"If Leroy was gone someone would still have to get past an usher who'd be right there by the door to the orchestra."

"Let's get a name," Mickey said.

We found Jose Zambrini on the telephone in the lobby box

According to St. John

office. He hung up when he saw us. We asked for and he gave us the name of the usher. Carol Brown, a drama student at San Francisco State. "She'll be working the Sunday matinee tomorrow."

"We do not want to wait that long," the Chief said.

Jose wrote down her number for us.

When we got back to the office I called Ms. Brown at home. A Mrs. Brown told me her daughter was out and not expected until very late.

"We'll have to take in the matinee."

The Chief groaned. Mickey sighed. And even I wasn't all that thrilled about it.

There was a message on the tape. The voice was a high-pitched male's. It asked for a call back as soon as possible.

"He's mine," Mickey said.

"What about me?" Chief Moses asked.

"What about the play tomorrow?"

"Damn," Mickey said, "I'll call him on Monday."

Even though we were reluctant, we all knew we should be there for the Sunday matinee. Just in case.

12

I drove over after lunch on Sunday and met Mickey and Chief Moses in the theater parking lot. There was still an hour to curtain time but the lot was full. I had to squeeze the T-Bird into a tight space that wasn't legal.

"We have trouble," the Chief said.

In front of the theater there was a crowd of people and it took me a moment to sort it into appropriate groups. The easiest to spot were the police in their blue uniforms. They had set up barricades on the sidewalk to keep two other groups safely separated: the pickets and the theatergoers.

The pickets were marching back and forth in front of the lobby doors. There were about two dozen of them all together, with about two-thirds female. Everyone was carrying a hand-lettered sign. Most of the women marchers also had at least one small child in tow. A few women carried infants in papoose carriers at their chests. The signs ranged from "No Bail for Killers" to "Stop Nudity

In Plays"—this latter by members of a group named SNIP. Sometimes those acronyms work.

Today there were three TV vans and a half-dozen reporters for the pickets to play to. One woman and her child were being interviewed on tape for the evening news by a local anchor.

The cops were at the barricades keeping the pickets separated from the line of ticket purchasers. Under their white riot helmets they looked bored as hell. They weren't expecting any real trouble from these people.

The line for tickets was long, wrapping around the building and continuing along its side. Opening night was nothing like this. Denny's sleepwalk had been described in detail by every crime reporter in the city in his or her account of the murder. Nobody cared how relevant it was. Everyone knew it made great copy. The local headlines ended up reading like they had been written for the *National Enquirer.*

The publicity surrounding Amanda Cole's death had also helped. The idea of seeing a possible real life lady Macbeth performing the role must have intrigued the city's theatergoers and, from the looks of some of the strange types in the line, some others who had never been to live theater before.

The line moved ahead, undulating like a Chinese New Year's dragon on parade. The pickets weren't hurting ticket sales at all.

We got into the much shorter will-call line and picked up our comps. I looked at where we were sitting. Not as close to the stage as opening night, but it had to be a sellout today.

Ticket stubs in hand, we went in search of the female usher who had been near the entrance to backstage the night of the murder.

A young woman with bushy mouse brown hair and eyes so blue she had to be wearing tinted contact lenses came up to the three of us. She was about five feet four in her low black pumps, and busty beneath her tuxedo jacket. She took our ticket stubs and handed us each a program. Denny's face was on the cover.

She started to open the doors to the orchestra when I asked, "Ms. Carol Brown?"

She was startled. "Yes?"

I explained who we were and asked her to answer a few questions. She had already talked to the cops but she agreed as long as it didn't interfere with her work.

According to St. John

"No problem," I said.

Waiting behind us was a couple who were dressed more for an opening night than for a Sunday matinee. She led them through the doors and we waited. When she returned I asked her about her routine during the performance.

"When it begins the doors to the orchestra are shut. Late arrivals are seated only during breaks between scenes."

"So you stand out here waiting?" Moses asked.

"Uh-huh," she said, bending her neck to look up at him.

"Then you can see Leroy by the entrance to backstage?" I asked.

She blinked those tinted eyes and shrugged. "I guess so. Some of the time at least."

"When the man is there," Chief said.

"But not all of the time?" Mickey asked.

"I'm not looking for him. I'm busy."

"So you might not notice if he disappears," I said.

"It's very possible."

"Where is Leroy now?" the Chief asked.

She looked over at his stool. It was empty and she hadn't noticed. "Probably backstage. You never know with him."

"On the night of the murder was Leroy at the door?" Mickey asked.

"On and off. I guess. I couldn't swear to it."

"That night did you notice anyone going backstage from here?" I asked.

"No."

"Are you sure?" The Chief pressed.

"I didn't see anybody. I told that to the police."

I gave her my card in case she remembered something.

"Were there latecomers to seat?" I asked as she pocketed the card without looking at it.

"There always are."

"So between scenes you were seating people."

"Sure. There's a line now. I've got to seat you."

"We'll wait," Mickey said. "I want to use the powder room."

Mickey went into the restroom across from the doors that Carol guarded. Carol started seating people in the orchestra again. The Chief and I stared at Leroy's empty stool. When Mickey came out Carol led us to our seats. Farther back but at least on the aisle.

113

"What did that get us?" Mickey asked as we settled in.
"It expands the possibilities of opportunity. Next I'll talk to Leroy."
"That may call for the Great Tracker," The Chief said.
Every seat around us was taken. I looked up at the balcony. The audience in front was hanging over the railing.
This audience was unusually raucous, more like the crowd at a Warrior basketball game. Or like the groundlings in Shakespeare's day.
"This isn't a play. This is a media event," I said.
"Are you complaining?" Mickey asked.
"I'm missing the 49er game."
"I'm sure you'll find something interesting enough here," she said. "Anyway it's just the last scab game." The football strike was over and the real teams would be back on the field next weekend.
"I told you. That's what I like about those games. Guys off the street playing in the pros."
The audience was getting impatient and louder. There were cat-calls and whistles and some nasty comments about Denny.
The people in the row in front of us, mostly young men in dark suits and ties and young women in frilly dresses, were whispering intently among themselves. They looked like they were out on a church-sponsored field trip. I stood up to remove my coat and to get a better look at them. They all had rolled up posters on their laps or at their feet.
"Keep an eye on this group in front of us" I said to the Chief.
He nodded.
It was still fifteen minutes until curtain time. If I was going to get a chance to talk to Leroy it was now. If he had appeared.
"Be right back," I said. Carol was examining a ticket and I slipped by her to the wing that had the entrance to backstage. The elusive Leroy Washington was sitting on his stool.
He seemed cold sober.
"Can't come in here, man," he said.
Leroy was a coal-skinned black in his sixties. He had gray curly stubble on his head that matched his beard. His broad flat nose flared out below custard-colored eyes. He had on a gray outfit that looked more like a chauffeur's uniform than a doorman's. I didn't smell any whiskey on his breath, but it wasn't even two o'clock in

According to St. John

the afternoon. Maybe Leroy only drank when the sun went down.

I showed him my I.D. Always impressive.

"I done talked to the cops already." He scratched his head.

"I'm a private investigator. I'm trying to help Miss Belknap."

"Nice Lady. Not like that other one."

Another friend of Amanda's. "Were you on duty here opening night?"

"Suppose so. Be my job."

"So you were out here up until the intermission?"

He looked away and said, "Sure, man."

"The whole time."

He hesitated. "Most a the time."

I gave him a way out. "Were you feeling okay?"

"I do believe I was havin' a bad night."

"What do you mean?"

He raised his custard eyes to me. "Somethin' I ate. Give me the trots somethin' awful."

"You tell that to the cops?"

"I tol' the cops I don't see nobody get by. An I don't." He licked his dry lips.

I slipped Leroy a five to keep on good terms with him. I didn't bother giving him a card.

"Somebody else been askin' questions," he said as I started to turn away.

"Who?"

"White boy. Like you."

"Give you a name?"

"Nope. Jus' this card."

The card he showed me was my own. The sonofabitch P.I. was pulling my own trick on me.

"Shit," I muttered. I was looking forward to meeting this clown. In a dark alley.

I got back to my seat just as the house lights were dimming.

"Saw Leroy." I said.

"Guarding backstage?" the Chief asked.

"So far."

At Denny's first appearance there were a few wolf whistles and catcalls from the back of the orchestra and from the balcony.

But things were relatively quiet through the intermission. The audience began to act up as we approached the nude scene. There were burlesque calls from the back to Denny to "Take it off!" There were more wolf whistles.

It was time for the sleepwalk.

I half expected Denny to be wearing a nightgown. But no. I admired her gutsiness.

As she began to deliver her lines the audience grew quiet. But not for long.

Suddenly the young people in the row in front of us popped up and started shouting religious slogans about the abominations of lust. At the same time they were unrolling the posters they had brought. Then they began to chant: "Shut down Satan's work! Shut down Satan's work!"

I assumed the posters said much the same thing.

Ushers rushed down the aisles but Mickey, the Chief, and I were right on top of it. Each of us got at least two of the clean-cut protesters by the backs of their necks and sat them down. Then we moved along our aisle and put down the rest of them. They complained. They claimed First Amendment free speech rights and religious freedom.

"I do not recognize the white man's constitution," Chief Moses said.

Someone complained about police brutality.

"We are not the police," the Chief said.

"We just want to see the play," Mickey said.

"And you were blocking our view with your signs and making it impossible to hear with your chanting. You're infringing on our ticket rights," I said.

They grudgingly settled down.

"Enjoy the play," I said and I suspected the young men would, despite their concern with abominable lust.

We had intimidated the hell out of a row of troublemakers and were having an effect on the whole theater as well.

I thought that Denny stopped to smile at us. The play went on without further incident.

Except that Carol brought a note to us that read: "Come to my office after the play, P. Maydik."

Exactly the man we were planning to talk to next.

After waiting through numerous curtain calls we made our way

According to St. John

to Maydik's office. It was directly backstage, near the prop shop, the width of the stage and three corridors away from the private dressing rooms at the rear of the building. The door was wide open. There was a desk for a secretary but no one was at it. Maydik was sitting alone in a windowless office.

"I wanted to thank you," he said.

"We wanted to ask you some questions," I said.

"I know. I've heard."

Maydik was classically handsome with a large head and a sharp profile. He wore his hair in a short natural Afro that was thick and dark except for touches of gray at the temples.

When he stood up I could see that he was at least six feet tall. His dark eyes took in the three of us. Then his lips curved into a smile beneath slightly flared nostrils. The teeth he showed were perfect and his handshake was firm and dry.

The three of us took up all the empty seats in the office, including the one behind the secretary's desk. The room was filled with yellow filing cabinets and little else. On a corner of Maydik's desk was a clean glass ashtray. There were two framed play posters on the wall but no gallery of Maydik pictures posed with the stars of the theater. I liked that.

"You did a good job on those fanatics," he said.

We nodded in agreement.

"Good thing you were all here."

"Sometimes it is wise to travel as a tribe," the Chief said. Maydik just looked at him.

"Other times we go our own separate ways. It's a more efficient use of labor," Mickey said.

Maydik settled back into his large executive chair, the only touch of luxury in the office. It was time for Twenty Questions.

I started with the familiar. "You wanted Amanda out?"

"Why?" he shot back.

"Because you wanted an interpretation based on the sexual relationship between Macbeth and his Lady. You wanted the nude sleepwalk. Amanda wouldn't have any of it."

"There are always artistic differences between a star and a director."

"Did you try to replace her?" Mickey asked.

"I talked about it."

"With whom?"

"Mr. Julian Kismodel. Our producer. He showed me her contract. There was a large buy-out figure. She had me."

"Didn't you have any authority?" Mickey asked.

He rolled his eyes and did a partial turn of his chair. He was showing us a chiseled profile.

"There's more. Amanda had artistic control in her contract."

"Who got her that kind of deal?"

"Her agent. A real bitch."

"Somebody had to sign it," the Chief noted.

"Not me. No way. The producer bought it. Kismodel. He wanted her."

"Was her salary large?" I asked.

"Yes. Julian is generous. Now how about some sherry?"

We accepted. Might as well keep it civilized.

Maydik reached down to the lowest filing drawer of one of the cabinets and pulled it open. Glass rattled against metal. I looked down and saw a Llama pistol.

He followed my eyes and said, "The gun seems to have slid forward. If you're wondering there are still places in America where blacks are not appreciated playing white parts. After a run-in with the Ku Klux Klan in rural Georgia I bought myself some protection. Fortunately, I've never had to use it."

He shoved the gun back into the rear of the filing drawer.

"Now about the promised sherry."

Maydik took a bottle of a Spanish brand I didn't recognize out of the same drawer. Four stemmed glasses appeared on his desk. He poured and let us each take a glass.

I sipped the sherry. It was excellent.

"Why did you go back to Amanda's dressing room?" I asked.

"To see how she was feeling."

"How long were you back there?" Mickey asked.

"I was with her for less than a minute. Just long enough to see that she was dead."

"But not enough time to kill her?" the Chief asked.

Perry Maydik spun the chair. His lips were pursed in anger. But he said, "I will let that pass. I was backstage with the crew and actors the entire time. Except for less than five minutes."

Five minutes. It wasn't much. And without much of a viable motive.

According to St. John

"And you just wanted to see how she was doing?" I asked.

"I wanted to talk to her about changing her approach. Now that we were opening with my interpretation."

"But she was dead when you got there," Mickey said.

"The lady was gone."

"What did you do?" the Chief asked.

"Called 911 Emergency. What else could I do?"

There were several more specific items I was interested in. "Has there been another P.I around asking questions?"

"No. Just the police."

"How was the company doing financially?"

"Theater always has its problems."

"Who handles the books?" the Chief asked.

Maydik finished his sherry and put the glass back down on his desk. He wrinkled his brow. "Biggs Accounting. Biggs, Black and Black."

"Two final questions?" I asked.

"Yes?"

"Was Kismodel involved with Amanda Cole?"

Maydik bit his lower lip. He picked up the empty sherry glass and twirled it between his fingers. "I don't know," he said.

"It could explain why he treated her as he did," Mickey said.

"Julian makes it a habit of getting the biggest star available. For that he always pays," the director said.

"Were you sleeping with Denny Delknap?" I asked suddenly.

"No," he said without emotion.

"Amanda Cole claimed you were."

"She was a crazy woman when it came to young actresses."

"A lot of people didn't like that crazy woman," I said.

"I know. But I was not one of them. She annoyed me but she was a professional. I admired her even if I didn't agree with her."

"What's eating Ullwanger?" I asked.

"He's been depressed since we opened. Worse than ever. But who knows?"

There seemed to be another question to ask but I couldn't think of it. I looked to my partners for help but I didn't get any. Only a comment from the Chief.

"You could use a few windows. Let in some sunlight."

Maydik shook his head. "I detest the sun."

We looked at him.

Maydik didn't explain.

"Thank you for your help, Mr. Maydik," I said.

We left Perry Maydik sitting alone in his windowless office just like we found him.

When I got back to the office there was a message to call Denny.

"Thanks for the rescue," she said.

"That's what good detectives are for."

"Can I buy you all dinner? To pay you back."

"There's a problem with that. I'm the only one here."

"Sometimes you have to settle for what you can get. Can I buy you dinner?"

"You bet," I said. "Rewards are gratefully accepted."

Denny picked the restaurant, a place where only naturally raised meats, poultry, and fish were served. Guaranteed free of steroids and chemicals. Vegetables were said to be organically grown in Sonoma County. Smoking was outlawed. The place was owned and operated by some far eastern religious sect.

"You brought us to a place where you can't smoke?" I asked.

"I've got to give it up."

We sat on a wooden elevated area from which we could see the chefs at work in a glass-enclosed kitchen.

The only problem was getting a waiter. All of them seemed to be great friends with the customers in the front part of the restaurant where they were hanging around and talking. While I signaled for a chatty waiter to come over and take our order Denny said, "That incident today upset me more than I can say."

"You didn't show it."

"I'm an actress. But if you weren't there . . ."

"But we were." Where was the waiter? My arm was getting tired and I was getting pissed.

"What if it happens again?"

"I don't expect a repeat."

She took my hand. I stopped signaling. Her perfect nails were painted red. "What if there is? Can't you be there?"

A flowery fragrance drifted across the table from her dark hair. "Not every night. Much as I might like to."

"Please, Jeremiah," she purred.

According to St. John

I was losing. Then I lost. "Oh what the hell. But only for a week."

The waiter arrived. I wasn't pissed anymore.

We both ordered crabcakes with avocado salsa and I got a bottle of Landmark Chenin Blanc.

"I heard there's been some other investigator asking questions," she said.

"So did I. I figure I'm going to run into him sooner or later. In fact I can hardly wait."

But why hadn't Perry Maydik heard about him?

13

On Monday, exactly one week after Mickey's Columbus Day announcement that we were all going to see her friend and ex-roommate Denny Belknap act in *Macbeth*, I was preparing to take on Biggs, Black and Black to try to find out the financial condition of the Marina Theater Company.

The Chief spent the morning on the phone pursuing his search for the missing pair of Slater and son. He found out that Slater's girlfriend was addicted to Bingo.

"A gift from the Great Spirit," the Great Tracker said. "I must warn you. The phone bills will be large."

"Cheaper than airfare," I said. "And we're not paying anyway."

"True."

The Chief wasn't a great fan of flying. He'd rather do his tracking on the good earth.

He started his calls with the Seminole game in Collier County, Florida, and worked north and west from there.

I went through my collection of business cards twice, trying to come up with a credible role to play at the accounting firm. I came up with one but none of my cards would do.

Mickey called the client with the high-pitched voice. He wanted to come in to talk to her this morning. I left her waiting for him and headed to a desk-top printing operation on Van Ness.

Michael, the proprietor of the publishing operation that specialized in customized business cards, stationery, and letterhead saw me coming through the glass storefront. He met me at the door dressed in blue farmer's overalls and high red sneakers with the tops flapped down.

Michael was in his twenties but he had already lost most of his hair. He had spent two years at Stanford studying computer science and going bald before he decided to make money, which he was now doing. The place was called Wings for some reason and it was always crowded.

Michael, who had seen me work before, looked around uncomfortably, and then directed me to an empty computer station as far away as possible from his other customers. I appreciated the privacy. I went to work. In twenty minutes I had the letterhead stationery and business cards I wanted. I knew Michael didn't want to see them.

I paid in cash on my way out and asked, "Why is this place called Wings anyway?"

"That's my name, Mr. St. John." Sometimes the easiest answers are the right ones. I wrote that down in my book of P.I words to live by. Maybe they could help me in the Denny Belknap case.

I left the store and walked back to the office with everything I needed for the assault on Biggs, Black and Black.

At the office Chief Moses was still on the phone. He was working on North Dakota. I looked at the log of the calls he had made and whistled.

Mickey was in my office, sitting at my desk.

"Something wrong with your desk?" I asked.

She scowled. Blond hair fell over one eye. She didn't brush it back.

"The guy with the voice showed up," she said.

I sat down on my couch.

"Out with it. What's bothering you?"

According to St. John

She tilted her head forward, still blind in one green eye. "The client is a young man of the gay persuasion who has to go out of town for a few weeks. He wants to make sure that his lover isn't running around on him while he's gone. He is terrified of catching AIDS. He and his partner have regular blood tests and they are both clean."

"And your job is to see if the partner left behind stays clean." I put my hands behind my head and looked up at the ceiling. There were some interesting ethical questions here.

Brushing her hair back, Mickey said, "I tried to explain that while we can prove infidelity there is no guarantee that we won't miss a liaison."

"What did he say?"

"That he knew that."

"Did you take the case?" I asked. Mickey was not one to turn away paying clients.

"Jesus, I hate that kind of peeping."

"And you can't exactly count on a video camcorder."

"I can cover the house where they live with a camcorder. That's a start."

"How about tailing him to gay bars? You'll be safe there at least. But hard to keep up a cover. Maybe play it as a transvestite. At least the gay bath houses have been closed down."

"Shit, Jeremiah. I don't like it. I can't promise to deliver what the client wants."

"Don't take the case."

She tossed her head back. "Too late." She held up a check. "I'm thinking computers."

"What's the client's name?" I asked.

"Let's just call him Vincent."

"Why?"

"His request."

"He lives in the Castro?" I asked.

"Where else?"

I stood up and moved towards my desk, a subtle hint that I was ready to reoccupy it. "When do you start with the Vincent case?" I asked.

"At least it's not until he leaves the city tomorrow."

I spread the materials from Wings Publishing on my desk.

"Good. You can help me with Biggs Accounting this afternoon."

She stood up. "Using this stuff?"

"Sure."

She came around the desk. "No way. That's illegal."

"Just because you used to be a cop . . ." I was saying as she left the room for her desk.

I started typing a letter of introduction for the both of us on my fresh illegal stationary.

By one o'clock Mickey was bored enough to give it a shot. We kept a wardrobe for Mickey—with outfits ranging from professional businesswoman to amateur hooker—in a closet in my office in case she needed a disguise. Like now.

"Try the hooker costume," I suggested.

"Dream on, Jeremiah."

She took out a dark business suit, white ruffled blouse, and low black pumps. When she emerged from the bathroom she was perfect. She was even wearing her oversized frames with the clear glass lenses. All she needed to do to look the part was to purse her lips and wrinkle her brow. I put on a blue blazer which Mickey said was fine for the part. And she liked the yellow paisley tie.

"Do I look Washington?"

"Sure," Mickey said.

She looked at the letter and our business cards. The letterhead said The National Endowment for the Arts with their Washington, D.C., address. The cards listed us as NEA Grant Proposal Reviewers. "Do you really think this will work?"

"Sure," I promised.

We left the Chief at work on the telephone and headed downtown to Biggs, Black and Black. Timing was all-important so we took the T-Bird. After parking on the fifth floor of a high rise garage we got to the accounting office just after two o'clock Pacific Time. By then the National Endowment for the Arts Office running on Eastern Time would be closed and no one could check us out with a telephone call until tomorrow morning.

Our cards got us immediate assistance from a blue-haired secretary who had to be approaching retirement age. The name on her plate was Lotta Tyral. She reached one of the Mr. Blacks on the intercom and told him who we were. He agreed to see us.

According to St. John

I winked at Mickey. We had taken the right approach. As NEA representatives, we were here to give the Marina Theater Company money, not take it away. Doors opened for us.

Lotta informed us that this Mr. Black was handling the theater account.

We went into a small office, much smaller than any attorney's I've ever seen. There was a neat metal desk, a calculator on one corner of it and family portraits on the other. The In-basket was empty, the Out-basket full. Lotta needed to get in there soon.

The view was of an office building next door. I could see a very pretty brunette sitting at her desk working by a window directly across from Black's. There had to be some compensation for not getting to see the bay or either bridge. I wondered if Black ever tried to make contact with her.

Black was dressed in a tweed jacket with elbow patches that made him look more like a university professor than an accountant. He had tweed hair that matched his jacket, horn-rimmed glasses, a round pink face, and smooth cheeks that didn't have to see a razor often. I figured he was Black Junior.

Mickey and I took moderately comfortable chairs after I gave Black our cards and my letter of introduction from an Assistant NEA Director whose name I had lifted from a Washington Directory. Nothing like authenticity.

"I recognize the name," Black said.

"I was sure you would," I said.

Black was looking at Mickey and not really paying much attention to me. Then she crossed her legs and even her severe suit looked sexy. She was doing her job. In this kind of situation it is better to have the mark distracted.

"What can I do for you?" he asked.

"The Marina Theater Company has put in a proposal for substantial NEA support. The Marina is the kind of operation we at NEA would like to fund. But we have to confirm their financial situation before we can go ahead with the grant."

"I'll have to call Washington," he said without missing a beat. We were prepared for that.

"Go right ahead," Mickey said and smiled.

He smiled back and turned apologetic. "It's one of our standard procedures."

Mickey winked at him. "We understand procedures if anyone does. You have to, to survive in D.C."

Black nodded and punched in the number on his phone. We waited.

"It's too late back east," he realized. "It's just a recorded message," he said as he hung up.

"Damn," Mickey said as she looked at the watch. "This can't wait. We're leaving tonight for Minneapolis."

"The Guthrie?" he asked.

"Oh, you know theater then," she said.

"Of course. That's why I handle this account."

"It would be a shame to lose this funding on a deadline technicality," I said.

"Could there be an extension?" he asked. The man was concerned which was a good sign for us.

"Impossible," Mickey said.

Black stood up. "I'll try to reach Mr. Kismodel. But that's not always easy."

"No. No. At this point the review is confidential. It's your cooperation we're counting on. We have an unaudited statement from Mr. Kismodel. What we need is a confirming audit statement."

He sat back down. "And this is a significant grant for the theater?"

"Oh, yes," Mickey purred.

"Did you see their *Macbeth*?" I asked.

"Twice," he said and then turned to look out of the window. I was sure he exchanged a look with the woman in the window of the building across the way. I had hope for Mr. Black.

"What the hell. You are the government. What do you need?" We had him. I smiled at Mickey. She had done a good job.

"We fund theaters that need support," I said.

"You mean ones that are losing money."

"Usually," Mickey said.

He went to the computer in the corner of the office, called up the Marina Theater account, and ran off a hard copy on a printer.

"In your terms you've got a winner here."

We looked at the spread sheet. With a little assistance from Black we saw that the theater company was losing money. Big money. A disastrous production would damage it severely. Maybe

According to St. John

even shut down the company. Maydik was in deep shit. He needed a hit. And Kismodel was losing his symbolic shirt as producer.

"They certainly could use a grant," I said.

"They could use something," Black said, "they're a quarter million in the red."

"A nice round sum," Mickey said.

We thanked Black who had turned out to be an okay guy for an accountant. I hoped things went well for theater in San Francisco for his sake. And I wished him luck with the woman across the way. He blushed.

Too bad the NEA was going to have to turn down the Marina Theater request. We left to ransom my car from the parking garage.

On the drive back to the office Mickey said, "Maydik is a better possibility now. Money is a real motive."

"One of the best. And then there's Julian Kismodel, producer," I said. I spotted a parking space and beat two other cars to it. One of the drivers blew his horn angrily at me. I ignored him.

"Nice job," Mickey said.

"Yeah. And it's only four blocks from the office."

As we walked uphill on Octavia I said, "But there are easier ways to get out of a contract than murder."

"You're right. There's something missing," Mickey said.

"It'll come to us."

"Who's going to bring it?"

"I have a feeling we'll be meeting up with a certain snooping P.I. very soon. He just might have what we want."

The Chief was gone when we got back. He had left no message. Just the answering machine on.

Mickey decided to start her job for Vincent in the Castro.

"I'm going to go over to his place and set up the video camcorder. I'm going to have to rent a van to house it."

"Do what you have to."

"It's shitty work," she said.

"I know, but you took it."

"Don't remind me." The swirl of hair came over her eye. She brushed it back and sighed. "It's impossible to guarantee innocence."

"We do the best we can in this imperfect business. Just like in the law."

"If he's running around on Vincent I hope he does it right away." She went to change out of her NEA bureaucrat business suit.

After Mickey left I went upstairs and looked in my refrigerator. There were some deli leftovers. I passed.

I called Denny. It was Monday and the theater was dark but there was no answer.

I wondered about Denny and her ex-husband. And about her and the handsome Perry Maydik who was in a position to do all kinds of career favors for her. And I still thought about that private dressing room she had as an understudy.

Then I thought just about Denny. I settled for deli leftovers and a loneliness I didn't really mind.

14

After all of that transcontinental effort on the telephone, Chief Moses ended up spending the rest of the week traveling around California from Bingo game to Bingo game in his pickup.

Mickey was busy with her video camcorder, her rented van, and the wanderings of Vincent's boyfriend. He led her to a lot of places she wouldn't have wanted to be caught dead in. She also complained that she couldn't catch him with any other man.

"Which would mean I could call Vincent and get off this damn job," she said.

"Keep trying," I said.

"I will," she promised as she went to check the results of eight hours of camcorder surveillance of Vincent's house.

But when she got back it was no luck again. Maybe Vincent did have a faithful lover.

As promised I was on duty at the theater. I got to see enough productions of *Macbeth* to last several lifetimes. Even Denny's sleepwalk lost its fascination. In fact, I fell asleep after the intermission twice and slept right through it.

On Tuesday night there were a few pickets and some hecklers in the audience. But the rest of the patrons hushed the hecklers. By Wednesday everything had cooled down. No pickets and no hecklers. Just packed houses every night.

During the day I did my work for Forsander and Samaho. I talked to every member of the cast, the crew, the ushers, the ticket takers, the box office people, the custodians, and the house manager and the stage manager. I talked to Leah X. I talked to Perry Maydik again. And to Leroy. So far everyone but the unreachable Julian Kismodel who his secretary informed me was in Stratford, Canada, at the Shakespeare theater.

Everyone told me they had said it all to the cops before. Everyone told me that Amanda Cole was a bitch. As popular with the actors as broken glass on the stage during a performance of *Oh! Calcutta*.

I tried to pin down the identity of the other P.I. but decided that he hadn't let anyone on to who he really was. I did get a good enough description to know him if I saw him around.

I was looking for a short and stocky man who was running to fat. He was bald and had a round ruddy face. Everyone who saw him said he had on a tan belted raincoat—just like in the movies.

By early Thursday I was getting to be a pain in the butt. I didn't mind that. Sometimes it just comes with the territory. Especially when you're learning a few things. Like the name of the theater Candy Man—who had not been seen since the night of the murder. I found out from a young actress who pleaded for a confidentiality I promised to maintain as long as possible that Leah X. hated both Amanda and Denny because she believed Maydik was "porking" both white women. And that she had seen Leah slip out of the backstage area and go to the dressing rooms during the first act.

She also suggested that Leroy knew more than he was saying, which led me back to the reluctant dragon at the gate.

I pushed an uncomfortably sober Leroy once more. He looked in bad shape. The stubble was longer and it looked dirtier. The custard yellow eyes were badly bloodshot. He was shaking so much I was afraid he would fall off his stool.

"Did you see anyone going backstage before Mr. Maydik?"

According to St. John

"Ain't supposed to say."

"You said you didn't see anyone. Why are you changing your story?"

He held out one dark trembling hand. "It Thursday, man."

"And no pay till Friday."

"Pretty smart for a white boy." He gripped the seat of the stool with both hands, like he felt it was spinning under him.

Maybe it wasn't exactly ethical to use his addiction but what the hell. I slipped him a twenty. He grunted but nodded.

"Three bottles a medicine," he said.

"Who went back there?"

He scratched his chin. "Mr. Julian."

"Kismodel?"

"Be him."

"Did you tell the cops?"

"Cops don't buy no nigger man booze."

"Did he usually go backstage?"

"He usually not aroun'."

"How long did he stay?"

"Fifteen. Twenty minutes."

"Didn't Kismodel tell you to keep it quiet?"

"Sure did. Give me couple bottles a Harper. But they gone."

If we ever went to trial we would have a surprise witness or two to ambush the prosecution with. The only problem was proving either Leah X. or Kismodel actually entered Amanda's dressing room that night. But at least we had some ways of creating reasonable doubt in the minds of a jury.

I bumped into the house manager Jose Zambrini and decided to take another shot at him from a different angle. I had been concentrating on Amanda after she arrived. But I had some questions about that arrival.

"Mr. Zambrini, you were in the lobby when Miss Cole got to the theater that day?"

He tugged at his suspenders. "Yeah. She came right up to the front of the theater in a cab. She knocked on the glass doors and I let her in."

"I thought she had a key to the door by her dressing room."

"Yeah. She usually came in that way. She was the star."

"Why'd she come to the front?" I asked.

He snapped the suspenders and put the back of his hand to his forehead. "Who knows? She was sick."

"What did she say when you let her in?"

"I'm going to my dressing room. I don't feel well."

I found it strange that she hadn't gone directly there.

"Do you remember anything about the taxi?" Usually you can get the color if nothing else.

"It was yellow."

"A number?"

"You kidding?"

"Yeah."

I thanked Zambrini and went backstage to a phone to call Forsander. He was pleased by my discovery of what could be surprise witnesses. I felt like I was on a roll.

Then my roll came up craps. Almost. I ran into Johnny D. and an annoyed Oscar Chang in the lobby of the theater as I was leaving.

Detective Chang was as crisp and freshly pressed as ever. Johnny D. still looked like the before half of a dry cleaning ad.

"What are you doing here, St. John?" Chang asked.

"I've got a right. I'm an investigator for the defense."

He just glared at me with those dark eyes. "You better not screw anything up. You better not tamper with witnesses. You better not mess with evidence. And you better not withhold evidence. Got that?"

"Oh I got it," I said.

Chang swore at me.

"Going to stay for the play tonight?" I asked. "Give your partner here some culture?"

"Can it, St. John," Johhny D. said.

As hard-ass as Johnny was trying to act now that he was in Homicide I managed to get him aside and ask him a few questions while Chang was off with Maydik getting another tour of the building.

"I gotta . . ." Johnny began.

"Just take a minute. First. You guys have got to see that there are other suspects."

"We got some people we're checkin' out. Your broad's not the only one. Just the best one."

"Second. Can you get me a list of the personal effects in Amanda Cole's room the night she was killed?"

According to St. John

"Shit." He looked around for Chang, who was nowhere in sight.
"Can you, Johnny?"
"Shit."
"We can formally petition for them," I said. "But I'm in a hurry."
"Who's not?"
"Can you?"
"I'll try. What're you lookin' for?"
"Keys. I want to know about her keys."
"Yeah. There were keys. What's the big deal?" Johnny was looking nervously around the lobby.
"I want to know what they were for."
"Oh."
"You guys did try them? To see what they opened?"
"Shit."
"You didn't?"
"I don't know."
"Can you get them out of the property room so we can try them out?"
"What's this 'we' shit?"
"It's my idea."
"What's the purpose?" he asked.
"You'll see." Since I wasn't sure, that was the best I could do.
"Without Chang?" he asked.
"It was his oversight too."
"I'll see what I can do."
"You know you can do it, Johnny."
"This better amount to somethin'."
"We'll open some doors at least. Or find some we can't."
He turned to leave.
"Wait, Johnny. One more question."
He narrowed his eyes.
"I need the name of the P.I who's been asking questions about the case."
He looked surprised. "Besides you and your partners?"
I nodded.
"I don't know, Jeremiah."
I believed him.
We both saw Chang and Maydik coming towards the lobby. I decided it was a good time to head for the parking lot.

On Friday I tried Kismodel again and found that he was back in the country. No longer unreachable. The secretary made an appointment for me that afternoon.

I had researched the man in everything from *Who's Who* to the *Chronicle's* pink theater section. He grew up in San Francisco and studied acting in New York City. There were some acting credits in New York but eventually he turned to directing and then producing. He liked to use "big name" stars in Shakespeare to bring in an audience. He was an entrepreneur and I wondered why he stuck with Shakespeare instead of going right for popular musical comedy and big bucks.

Of course he was independently wealthy, thanks to his marriage to the heir of a late San Francisco developer who gave us some of our ugliest architectural creations. Given those marital conditions, I wondered how independent he really was.

Unlike Maydik, Julian Kismodel had an elaborate office downtown. There was a receptionist, a secretary in her own office, and then Kismodel's space which was large enough to hold two of my offices. The walls were covered with framed theater posters and pictures of Kismodel with his stars. The man had a large slab of marble in free form for his desk and a high-backed executive chair that had adjustable and removable arms. Next to the desk there was one of those chairs that you knelt in to do your work. Supposed to be the latest thing in Scandinavian comfort. When I tried it once it reminded me of trying to kneel on a padded board in a church pew. Not one of my best childhood memories.

Where there were no posters there were bookcases, most of them containing plays grouped chronologically from early Greek tragedy through Shakespeare—who took up an entire bookcase—and one containing most of the contemporary playwrights from O'Neill to Miller to Mamet.

There was a large bust of Shakespeare on Kismodel's desk and smaller ones scattered about the office on tables along with Shakespeare pens, ashtrays, medals, paperweights and a coloring book. Besides the Shakespearean schlock there must have been fifty plants, ferns and ivy, hanging from the ceiling.

The only thing the office didn't have was a view. Kismodel Theatrical Enterprises was on the first floor and through the windows

According to St. John

you could see the street. Of course if you liked to people watch it wasn't bad.

"See anything you like?" the man asked from behind his desk.

"Sometimes I'm a little too obvious. Occupational hazard."

He nodded me towards a leather chair and I sat down.

"Sorry I couldn't see you sooner," he said, "but I had to complete negotiations with the Canadians."

"No problem."

When he had me sitting he stood up. He was about five foot nine and solidly built, with that oversized head you find on many male stage actors. The better to see them from the balcony. He had waves of brown hair running straight back from a high forehead, dark eyes, a wide aquiline nose, and an overly large mouth. He wasn't movie star handsome but I could easily imagine him on stage playing Julius Caesar. He was wearing elegantly cut jeans and a T-shirt with "Shakespeare Is the One" printed across the chest. He walked across his deep blue rug to one of the tables and picked up a yellow-bowled pipe. The bowl was carved into a likeness of Shakespeare. Then he sat back down, the pipe resting in the palm of his hand. There was a "No Smoking" sign on his desk over a picture of Shakespeare's tomb.

"You were losing money," I said getting right down to it.

"It happens in a lot of businesses." He got out a package of Sail tobacco and filled the pipe. When he lit it I didn't say anything. Hell, it was his "No Smoking" sign.

"But why stick to Shakespeare? There are easier ways to make money in the theater."

He puffed until he got the tobacco going. Shakespeare's crown was glowing red.

"I know that. But Shakespeare can sell. He was commercial in his time and he can be commercial today. Besides, I trained as a Shakespearean actor myself. I like to see his work on stage."

"But you were losing money with Amanda Cole."

"Advance sales were poor. But I expected that to change. But I'm not in it for the money. I'm bringing culture to the city. Paying it back more or less for what my late father-in-law put up here. I am a wealthy man."

"I know. Thanks to your wife's money."

That got to him. He asked abruptly, "What do you want to know?"

"Why you went backstage to see Amanda Cole the night she was killed?"

"I can deny that."

"I'm not the police."

"I can still deny it."

"I've got a witness."

He puffed angrily on Shakespeare.

"I went to talk to her about Perry's approach. The advance sales were terrible. Her name alone wasn't enough. We had to try something radical."

"Like nudity on stage."

"Maydik had a great success in London with a nude Desdemona during the death scene in *Othello*."

Kismodel was contradicting himself. Either he wanted to make money or he cared about the artistic product and culture. More likely he was hiding the real reason he went to see her.

"Were you sleeping with Amanda Cole?" I asked.

He rose up. "Get the fuck out of here."

"Did you provide fringe benefits—like cocaine—for your star performers?

"I said get the fuck out of here." He was coming around the desk towards me.

"Don't do anything we'll both regret."

He stopped.

"Thank you for your cooperation."

With Kismodel as possible lover I now had a possible jealous husband. Pretty soon I would have to make a list to keep up with all my suspects.

15

On Saturday I slept through the entire performance of *Macbeth*. It was the last one I promised Denny I would attend. If there was a problem with the audience it wasn't loud enough to wake me up.

My only excitement was kissing Denny goodnight—at the door to her apartment. She had been tired as hell from her performance. That was why she hadn't invited me in, I rationalized.

Now on Sunday I was missing the 49er-Saints game on TV. Some weekend.

I was missing the game because Mickey and I were driving out to Sausalito to see Parker Rinshell, the brand new widower. A friend that Mickey has at the phone company got us his unlisted number and a surprised Rinshell agreed to see us this afternoon. Obviously he wasn't a football fan.

As we crossed the Golden Gate Bridge I complained about missing the game.

"Put it on the radio," Mickey said.

"It's not the same."

"Use your imagination. Like you do on your cases."

"I'll try." I turned on the game. After a few minutes of listening to a 49er drive I said, "I miss the scab teams. The guys grabbing a few moments of glory. Now we have the pros back. The millionaire pros who asked the stadium vendors and ushers not to cross their picket lines."

"Of course the NFL Players' Union would honor their picket lines if they go out on strike."

"When artificial turf starts to grow," I said.

"Can I talk about my case while you listen to the game?" she asked.

"For you anything." she looked great in the Banana Republic mudcloth jersey she had on. It was one of two she owned. Today she was wearing the pumpkin colored one with a short dark skirt and Etruscan espadrilles. I always wondered what put her in a Banana Republic mood. Maybe it was travel. All the way to Marin County.

Mickey gave me a summary of the week she had spent tailing Vincent's lover and coming up empty.

"He's a health nut. Health food. Health clubs. Endless miles of jogging. And I had to follow him wherever he ran. I ache all over from the exercise and I'm hungry for real food. I'd say the guy is too worn out to have sex with anybody."

"So you can certify to Vincent that his partner is a good boy."

"He'll be delighted," she said.

"Tell him not to throw away his condoms. Just in case."

"Sure. I'll put it in the report under Advice to the Gay Male. Maybe include a few samples."

"Make sure you get the kind that come in rainbow colors," I said. I turned up the volume as the 49ers scored.

We climbed into the Sausalito hills, driving past trendy and expensive houses of wood and glass—always a lot of glass to capture the view—with BMW's and Mercedeses in driveways and under carports. At the top of a cliff we came to the address that Rinshell gave us. I spotted the number painted on the curb and pulled over. The only thing visible from the road was a locked garage and the flat cedar shake roof of the house and beyond that San Francisco

According to St. John

Bay and Angel Island. The day was clear with an intense blue sky and a warm sun. Nearly a hundred sailboats moved through the water. From here their sails looked like sharkfins.

A ferry was approaching the Sausalito landing below us. The bright sun gave the white metal a hot ceramic glow.

We went down two flights of newly repaired wooden stairs built into the side of the hill to get to an elaborately carved front door.

The house looked as expensive as any we had seen. I wondered what kind of car was locked in the garage up by the road. A Jag I bet.

We rang and identified ourselves to the voice on the intercom. Bolts were thrown and the door opened.

Parker Rinshell was dressed in an aqua cotton sweater, chino slacks, and docksiders sans socks. He was tan and maybe in good shape although way too thin for his six-four height. He looked like he ran a marathon a day and only ate frozen Gatorade. He had a long thin face that showed every bone—the kind of look a model tries for. His hazel eyes were large and sunken. His blond hair was cut very short to try to hide his hair loss. Obviously, on TV he had to wear a wig.

He extended a bony hand which we each shook.

Without a word he led us down a dim hallway to a heavy oak door. He opened it and ushered us into the most impressive library I had ever seen in a private home. The room was circular with mahogany book shelving running its entire height and circumference. There was six feet of shelving, then a column carved in relief in mahogany, then more shelving. This pattern was repeated around the room. And every shelf was full. It looked like you couldn't squeeze another book in anywhere. On each column there was a gold carriage light lamp. Above the shelves ran a wooden cornice that matched the columns. The circular dark blue ceiling was an astronomy chart of the night sky. A white globe light hung suspended beneath it like an indoor moon. There was a simple oak desk and matching chair, a reading lamp, and a wastebasket and telephone in the center of the library. There were three other chairs placed strategically around the room.

"Impressive," Mickey and I said together.

Rinshell downplayed it. "I like to read in comfort." He picked up a script from the desk and said, "I agreed to see you but I don't have much time." He waved the pages at us. "I'm studying this script for a commercial we're shooting this week."

Some excuse. How long does it take the man to memorize the lines for at most a sixty-second commercial? He wasn't exactly studying to play *Hamlet*.

"I understand. No small talk. We'll get right down to it."

Rinshell sat on the edge of the desk and Mickey and I pulled up chairs. He had the height advantage and the angle advantage on me. I balanced it out by letting Mickey start the questioning.

"Where were you the night your wife died?" she asked.

"In the audience."

"Did you go backstage to talk to her?"

"Of course. As soon as I heard she was sick."

"What time was that?"

"Well before the performance. I arrived early."

"Anyone who can confirm the time?"

"Why?"

"It makes a lot of difference. Did anyone see you backstage? Did you talk to anyone?" Mickey persisted.

"I stopped in to see Eric Ullwanger."

"Why?"

"Why? He's a friend of mine."

"You saw him before you went to your wife's dressing room?"

"Yes. He can confirm the time."

"Even though your wife was sick?"

He looked exasperated. "Yes. Is that so peculiar. Besides Amanda was always getting sick. I had to keep her various ailments in perspective."

"Then after you saw Ullwanger you went to see Amanda. How was she?"

"Obviously not well."

"What did she talk about?"

"Actually she kept going on about how Claudette Colbert had a skiing accident and lost the part in *All About Eve* to Bette Davis. She was feeling like an aging actress and she was drawing the obvious parallel."

Mickey switched gears on him. "Did she ask you for cocaine?"

"God no." He squirmed on the edge of the desk.

According to St. John

Mickey pushed on. "You'd think a husband would know about a cocaine habit."

"Sometimes they're the last to know," he said, with a defensive gesture of his skeletal fingers.

"That applies to some other things as well," I said as I stood up. I couldn't handle the height disadvantage like Mickey.

"What do you mean?"

"Was your wife faithful?"

"Of course she was. We'd been married for nearly twenty-five years."

"That's never a guarantee, and I've heard rumors."

"Rumors? That's how gossip columnists make their living. They fabricate stories to keep their readers interested."

"What abut rumors among the cast?" I asked.

"Jealousy." Parker Rinshell was more than annoyed. I didn't think we were going to last much longer.

"Now . . ." I began.

"I know what you're trying to do. You're looking for the jealous husband motive. Anything to get that Belknap woman who killed Amanda off. As I've said in other circumstances, the interview is concluded."

"I know. You've got to study your lines," I said.

"Exactly."

"Must be some commercial," Mickey said.

"Watch for it. We're shooting at the Pro Surfing Competition." He had missed her sarcasm by the length of a pipeline ride. Actors are like that.

He showed us out of the magnificent library and out of the house. On the way up the steps Mickey said, "I can't see that man surfing."

"Either he's a marathon runner in great shape or he's dying." There didn't seem to be any middle ground for Parker Rinshell.

We drove back to the office where I was hoping to catch the end of the game.

No such luck.

When we got there the front door was unlocked. I pulled out my S&W .38 and Mickey took her weapon out of her purse. I went in first, with Mickey behind me. We jumped across to the doorway that led to Mickey's office. I grabbed the .38 with both hands, spun into the room, and dropped to one knee. I could see directly into my office.

There was a man in a tan fedora sitting at my desk. His feet were up on it. When he saw me he slowly raised his arms over his head.

I got up, and with Mickey behind me, we went through the Chief's office into mine.

"You oughtta say 'Freeze' or somethin'," the intruder suggested.

"Thanks for the tip. I'll keep it in mind for the next time I find somebody breaking in. Now what the hell are you doing here?"

"I didn't want to sit out on the porch all day. I figured I'd come in and watch the game."

Then I noticed the sonofabitch had my TV out with the game on. Even though I didn't want to do it, I shut it off.

"Who are you?" Mickey asked.

"Name's Leo Stubbs," he said as he removed his hat with a flourish and tossed it at the coat rack. He missed but he acted like he had a ringer. "Can I put my hands down?" he asked.

"Yeah," I said, but I kept my gun on him. Mickey lowered hers.

Leo Stubbs had a full ruddy face with a snub nose, full lips, and a double chin. He was bald except for a curly fringe of black hair. Everything about him looked soft except for the eyes. They were hard and dark. He was wearing a tan belted raincoat that needed a trip to the cleaners and I could see holes in both of the soles of his unpolished black wingtips. He was the other P.I. The one who used my business card. The description I had fit him like skin.

"You're a P.I.," I said.

"Give that man a wooden nickel."

"I'll settle for you getting your damn feet off my desk."

"Glad to oblige." He swung them off. Sitting up straight in the chair he looked like he went about five six and maybe two hundred pounds. A barrel of fun. "Yeah," he continued, "I'm a P.I. Just like you two." He looked Mickey over with prurient appreciation.

"I hope not," Mickey said. She put her gun in her purse.

I holstered mine and asked, "How did you get in here?"

"You're kiddin'. I'm a pro and this setup ain't exactly on the cuttin' edge in office security systems."

We were vulnerable through the back window but that was still locked. And anyone coming through there would be likely to knock over my potted plant. My trap. I figured he used a credit card on the front door. A basic technique.

According to St. John

"What do you want, Stubbs?" I asked. I was sorry he hadn't run into the Chief. He wouldn't have been as patient with this clown as Mickey and I. [*I. ME OR as Mickey and I were*]

"We're workin' the same side of the street. I figured we could work together."

"By breaking in here?" I said.

"Consider it a security test. You flunked."

"An alarm system," I said to Mickey.

"After we get the computers," Mickey countered.

This wasn't the time to argue with her. I turned back to Stubbs. "First get out of my chair."

"Sure. Sure." He got up and took a client's chair. My height and weight estimate was on target.

I hoped he would try to smoke but I saw him look at my No Smoking sign.

I took my chair. Things were more or less back in order. If I had to ask the questions I had to be behind the desk.

Mickey sat on the couch.

Only I didn't get to do much asking.

"You're St. John and you're Michelle Farabaugh. Where's Chief Moses?"

"You did your homework."

"I'm a pro. Am I supposed to take that No Smoking sign seriously?" He reached into an inside pocket.

"You bet," I said.

Stubbs pulled out an empty hand.

"What's this side of the street we're both working, Stubbs?" I asked.

"Call me Leo."

"Not yet. I didn't appreciate your posing as me at the theater."

He shrugged. "An old P.I. trick. I got a collection of business cards. You probably got one too. If not you oughtta. No charge for the advice. Anyway we're both investigatin' the Cole broad's murder."

"Along with the police," I said.

"Yeah. But you and I got a different perspective from the cops. We know Belknap didn't do it."

"Who did?" Mickey asked.

"I got my suspects."

"They have names?" I asked.

145

He smiled yellowish teeth at me. He took his time. A master of the dramatic moment. Finally he said, "Maydik and Kismodel."

"You have a motive?"

"Yeah. They had key person insurance on Cole. A cool quarter mil. Just what they need to keep this theater of theirs afloat."

No wonder he avoided Maydik and probably Kismodel. He didn't want to tip them. I looked at Mickey. This could be something. "Which one gets the money?" I asked.

"They're partners. The Marina Stage Corporation with its two managing partners benefits."

So Maydik had not been straight with us. Assuming this P.I. knew what the hell he was talking about.

"What about Kismodel's money?" Mickey asked.

"It's his wife's."

That we knew. "So we have a motive," I said.

"Neat, ain't it? Could even be a conspiracy. That's what I figure it for."

I got up out of my chair and moved towards Stubbs. "You're working for the insurance company," I said.

He grinned. "Sharp as a fuckin' carpet tack." He looked at Mickey. "Sorry."

She waved her hand in dismissal. Stubbs's shift to gentlemanly concern struck me as absurd. The look on Mickey's face told me she took it the same way.

"The policy is with Hartman Life. I'm an investigator on retainer."

"You mean you're working for a company that doesn't want to pay off." I knew the work. We had performed it ourselves and it helped pay the bills.

"They're in business to make a profit. Not to get ripped off." He went for a cigarette again.

Mickey pointed to the sign. The ex-smoker was a true convert. Or maybe she was afraid of being tempted by the aroma of smoke in the air.

"A reflex," he said.

"How do we work together?" I asked. I wasn't sure I wanted to, but the man had come bearing the gift of a new and viable motive.

"You want to prove that Belknap is innocent. So do I."

"There's a subtle difference here," I said.

"What?"

"You want her innocent so you can pin the murder on the beneficiaries so they can't collect on the policy."

"Right."

"That's ass-backwards."

"Hey, St. John, they ain't payin' me to prove the fuckin' butler did it. They wanna save themselves payin' out this bonanza." No apologies for the language this time. This was the real Leo Stubbs emerging.

"And you get a bonus if you succeed."

"You bet your ass I do."

"Money motives all over the damn place," I said.

"Can we cut the bullshit? Do we work together or not?" He was halfway out of the chair, about ready to bump into me.

I looked at Mickey, who nodded and said, "Why not?"

"Why not?" I echoed. I dismissed the actual reasons I had for not working with Stubbs and decided that his help would be better than nothing.

"Then it's a deal?" he asked.

"It's a deal." We all shook on it.

"Now will you call me Leo?"

"Fucking-A," Mickey said with her wicked smile.

Leo laughed.

"It's Leo," I added.

"That's the spirit, Jerry."

"Jerry?" Mickey half-choked.

Jerry? No one had called me Jerry since high school. But what the hell. Jeremiah probably had too many syllables for Leo to handle. So I said, "Right on, Leo." We were in business.

We divided up the labor. Leo was going to concentrate on Maydik and Kismodel. We would take a more general approach with the other suspects.

"I can't accept the premise that it has to be one of the beneficiaries," I argued.

"It's both," he said.

"There are other leads to follow."

"You're wastin' your time. Money is the motive. Money always plays in fuckin' Peoria."

"You could be right. Consider us an objective check on your work."

"Horseshit."

WILLIAM BABULA

We spent forty minutes exchanging information about the case. Mickey ended up with a sheet of notes. Leo talked and listened. No note taking for him. In the end, except for the insurance policy, we didn't know much more than we did before. One puzzle piece at a time.

Later that evening I called Johnny D.'s number. I got Mrs. D., which meant Johnny was out, and worked my way through her Spanish and English to get my message through. She promised to tell him to call me.

A half-hour later he did. I chewed his ass off for holding out on the insurance information.

"You're the P.I.," he said. "Don't you like to discover things for yourself? More excitin' that way, I'd think."

"I'm not looking for excitement. I'm looking for some hard facts."

He sighed. "At least this is better, Jeremiah."

"What is?"

"Calling me at home."

"Keeps you out of trouble with Detective Chang?"

"Yeah. I'm on the eight-to-four shift. So you know."

"Except for overtime."

"The city can't afford overtime these days."

"I'll call you at home. No sweat. And if you're not there, I like talking to your beautiful wife. I get to teach her some English in the process."

"Screw you."

"English is the official state language of California, my *amigo*. Why keep her in ignorance?"

"What do you want, St. John?"

"I want to set up a time to try Amanda Cole's keys."

There was a long pause. "I can get them out of the property room tomorrow."

"When can we go to the theater?"

"Probably tomorrow evening. I'll call you, Jeremiah. Understand."

"Got it. By the way who won the 49er game today?"

"You didn't catch it?"

"I was busting my butt working."

According to St. John

"You're the detective. You find out." The sonofabitch hung up on me. I didn't mind. He gave me what I wanted. If keeping back a football score and hanging up a phone made him feel better about helping me, I couldn't complain.

I put on the news for the sports report. There's more than one way to skin a cop.

16

After a Monday morning trip downtown to invest some more of the brokerage house's money in the futures Carrie recommended, I was back in my office alone. My plan was beginning to work. I told Carrie that I had large amounts of money to invest but I felt futures were too risky. I suggested I was going to put everything I had in C.D.'s and tax-free bonds. The prospect of losing her client and her commission rattled her. She started talking about how stock index futures could be risk free and very profitable. When I thought she was going to reveal the scam she backed off. Which was okay with me. Next time I would come prepared to pull out. And I would be wearing a wire. Carrie would come through.

I knew the head of the house was getting impatient. He called me to tell me so. I assured him we were right on schedule. And now we were. Sometimes it takes a little while for truth to catch up to reality.

Mickey came in. She was dressed in a gray suit that made her look like a banker. It was the outfit she chose for her meeting with Vincent at a gay bar.

She would have been even safer in a bikini.

She told me Vincent had been ecstatic to learn the result of the tail and the camcorder surveillance.

"I told him we couldn't guarantee an AIDS-free lover but he wasn't listening. And then when he was writing the check for our services I stopped pointing out our limitations."

"Good business decision."

Mickey kicked off her shoes and collapsed on the couch.

"I'm tired. And I still ache from all that running and exercise."

"But you made a man happy."

"There are easier ways."

"You're telling me," I said.

"Don't start talking dirty to me, Jerry." She raised a fist from the couch.

We both laughed.

"I thought you liked it."

Before she bothered to reply the Chief came in. He had on his favorite outfit: jeans and his FSU T-shirt.

"How goes the search for Slater?" I asked.

Chief Moses settled into a chair and bit his lower lip. "I have leads. My gambling c3nnections came through."

"Where do you go now?" Mickey asked.

"Monte Carlo."

"I suggest you change into your three-piece suit."

"Come on," Mickey said.

"I am only going to Tahoe. I have four good leads to check out. And I want to beat the traffic."

"Before you drive off I want to tell you about a visitor we had yesterday." Then I told him, with an occasional interjection from Mickey, about Leo Stubbs.

When we were done the Chief was leaning towards violence against the man's person.

"Chief, he could come up with something for us," I said.

"Such men are dangerous because they know before they see."

"He brought us the insurance information and a motive for murder."

According to St. John

The Chief grunted then said, "Where the dog pees there is dog pee."

"Would you explain that?" I asked.

"Indian sayings are self-explanatory."

"Let's give Leo a chance, Chief," Mickey pleaded.

Chief Moses relented as he usually did when Mickey made a request. Beauty before anything was one of his golden rules. I wasn't sure what the others were.

After grabbing a handful of petty cash for the trip, he was gone in plenty of time to beat the rush hour of commuters going east on the Oakland Bay Bridge to Interstate 80 and the suburbs beyond.

Mickey said that she was exhausted, then added, "In this weakened state I can't fight you off."

The woman was flirting with me again. I took that as a good sign. But she left to take a cable car home, which I took as a bad sign.

It was Monday night so presumably Denny would be free. I called and invited her out to dinner.

"Come to my place," she said. "Cooking is just one of my many talents."

"Invitation enthusiastically accepted."

It was after four and I didn't have to be at Denny's until six. I called Johnny D. at home and this time got him.

"Yeah?" he asked, his voice surly as a Southern deputy sheriff's in a Burt Reynolds car movie.

"You ought to go into public relations for the force, Johnny," I suggested.

"Up yours, Jeremiah."

"Did you get Amanda's keys?" I didn't care what he said to me. What mattered was how he came through when I needed him.

"Yeah. Yeah. I got your damn keys."

"Let's try them out."

"What the hell. It's early. My kids are screamin'. I'll pick you up in fifteen minutes."

We rode in style in Johnny D.'s unmarked blue Plymouth, the stripped-down job that might as well have COP written across the doors and on the roof.

"I figure that Amanda came around to the front of the theater because she didn't have her key when she came back from lunch."

"What does that prove?" Johnny asked as he took a curve at fifty mph.

"Your driving proves you watch too many cop shows on the tube," I said.

"Just reruns of *The Streets of San Francisco*."

"It's possible that someone else could have had the key."

"Big deal," he said as he pulled in on a sharp angle next to a fire door behind the theater. "This the door?"

"Yeah." I got out of the car with the ring of keys. Johnny sat in the car with the motor running.

The third key opened the fire door. "Damn!"

"Kinda ruins your theory doesn't it?"

"Not exactly. I didn't really have one."

I went into the backstage area and tried the keys until I found one that fit Amanda's dressing room. That left five other keys on the ring. Two were car keys. Three looked like house keys. We would of course try the house in Sausalito. But after that?

I went out and got back in the unmarked car.

"Can I hang on to these?" I asked as Johnny pulled away, leaving a strip of the taxpayers' rubber down on the asphalt.

"Those keys are checked out to me. I'm responsible."

"Because of that I'll take extra good care of them."

He stopped reluctantly at a red light. "Defend 'em with your fuckin' life, Jeremiah."

"Yes, sir," I said and saluted.

Johnny pulled up over the curb in front of my office. Cop Power!

I had just enough time to shower and change for my evening with Denny Belknap—Lady Macbeth out on bail.

Her apartment off Lombard wasn't exactly the pad of a star. It was more like the loft of a starving artist. The drab furniture looked like it had been collected at Good Will and the St. Vincent DePaul Society. A few framed theater posters on the wall were the only real touches of color in the place.

Except for Denny. In contrast to her surroundings, Denny was beautiful. And colorful. Her dark hair glistened and her skin glowed pink. She was wearing a loose gold kimono with a large fire-breathing dragon embroidered in red and black and green on the

According to St. John

back. She was barefoot and didn't have much if anything on under the robe.

Besides being beautiful, she was cooking. I smelled tomato sauce simmering.

Denny had three cans of Olympia beer and a jug of red wine in her refrigerator. There was half a bottle of vodka under the kitchen sink. She poured herself a glass of red wine and offered me my choice of the lot. I stuck with a Henry's from the twelve pack I had picked up at a package store on the way over.

We sat down on the couch in the area that passed for the living room. We talked, but not about Amanda Cole.

A bottle of beer later I turned from our conversation to look around again. The place hadn't improved much.

There was the living room we occupied with its window looking out over the street, a bathroom, an eat-in kitchen, and a small bedroom right off the living room with a double bed, neatly covered with an orange and blue flowered spread. Splashes of color I had missed before.

Denny finished her wine and said, "Time to move into the kitchen."

I got another Henry's and refilled Denny's wine glass while she tossed a green salad. She served us while she kept an eye on a pot of boiling pasta. When it was done she dished it out with a thick tomato sauce, slightly sweet, and spiced with hot Italian sausage.

"You're right. Cooking is among your many talents."

She smiled mischeviously.

When we were done we retreated to the living room couch, leaving the dishes on the table.

Even though there were better things to talk about, I went to the topic we had been carefully avoiding so far. I asked about the night of the murder again.

We went over it twice. Denny couldn't remember anything new.

"One more time," I said. I was relentless.

She cursed me out.

"You're worse than the damn cops."

"They found what they wanted. I need something more. Something to get you off clean."

She went over it once more. She was drained. We just sat there in silence.

After a while I took her hand. "What about the jealousy angle? Parker Rinshell was backstage that night."

"I just don't know."

"Did she ever say anything about another man?"

"Not to me. Amanda and I were not exactly like sisters."

"Who was?"

"Who was what?"

"Close to her."

"Hmmm . . . Talk to Arden Booth. She took Amanda's death very hard. Still real upset by it. I guess they were friends. Arden's nice. Young. Attractive. But not threatening in any way to Amanda."

"Why not?"

"She doesn't have the talent."

"She was Lady Macduff?" I asked.

"Good. You remembered."

"One of the skills I try to develop. It helps in my line of work."

I recalled the reviews. Although she had been dismissed by Cleo Maura, she was at least noted as competent by the other reviewers. To me she had been convincing enough in her minor role for me to remember her name.

"Do you have an address?"

"I got it from her just before opening night. We were talking about getting together some evening. But after what happened, we never did."

I had spoken briefly to the woman on my pass through the cast and crew. Now I had something more specific to press.

Denny went into the bedroom and came back with Arden's address. No phone number. There was no phone yet.

She sat down on the couch again. This time quite a bit closer to me.

"Then she was just moving in?"

"I guess so. Do we have to talk about Arden? Do we have to talk about Amanda and everyone else anymore tonight?"

"You have any better subjects?"

Denny shifted on the couch. The flap of the kimono opened to reveal her white thighs and the tops of her breasts. Quickly she wrapped herself up. Even though I had seen her nude on stage all of those times I found her here to be extraordinarily erotic. Either it's true that some things should be left to the imagination or it was sexy because I wasn't sharing any of her with an audience.

I got her some more wine and me another Henry's. Before either of us was halfway through we found ourselves wrapped in each other's arms.

Shortly afterwards Denny was out of her kimono. Once again nothing left to the imagination.

"Your spirits are rising," she whispered.

Not only that. They were up and out.

I felt for my new wallet. The kind with the special plastic compartment for condoms. Another sign of the times. Which gave me pause.

I pulled back.

I tried: This was Mickey's best friend—or at least old good friend. I was in love with Mickey but the relationship wasn't going anywhere that I could tell. So what was I concerned about? Denny was beautiful and sexy. She obviously wanted to go to bed with me. She was also a woman I hardly knew. I couldn't deny the gnawing fear. There was the broken marriage with the unfaithful husband. There were the rumors of the affair with Maydik. The theater with its concentration of gays was an ideal breeding ground for the HIV virus. All you needed were a few infected bisexuals to cross the lines. I could see Chief Moses' point. The white man was ruining casual sex.

My spirits drooped right in her hand.

"What's wrong?" Denny asked, her eyes and moist lips turned up towards me.

"It doesn't seem right."

"What doesn't?"

"Us," I said.

"Are you thinking of Mickey?" she asked.

"Yes."

She stood up and wrapped herself in the robe. "Bullshit!"

"Huh?"

"It's not Mickey. I know what's bothering you. Fear. Fear of fucking AIDS."

That was an interesting way to put it. "No . . ." I began.

"No bullshit, Jeremiah. I'll give you my sexual history then you can make up your mind. I told you about my ex-husband running around on me. I didn't mention he was a bi did I.? No, I guess not. Well he was. He was making it with men as well as with other women. So did I take an AIDS test to see if I'd come in contact with the virus? That would be the sensible thing to do. If you want to fucking know! But I don't want to know! I can live with the uncertainty but not with knowing. My solution is to keep a basket of fresh latex condoms above my bed. Not very romantic but Goddamned practical. So here I am. Good fun in the sack but high risk on the Surgeon General's chart."

She was tempting as hell which meant it was time to get out of there. To get some time to think.

She looked at me as if she were reading my mind.

"I'd stay away from theater people too. No telling who they've been fucked by." She tied the sash of her robe.

I didn't know what to say. I tried, "I'm sorry." It seemed feeble to me.

"Don't be. Just leave." The tears were coming down, washing mascara and eyeliner in clown lines down her cheeks.

She deserved better. I got up and tried to hug her. Just to hold the woman.

"No. Please go."

I knew she meant it. As I opened the door she asked, "What are the odds Jeremiah. What are the fucking odds?"

I didn't know. I wasn't sure I wanted to. I closed the door softly behind me.

17

Tuesday morning Mickey called in sick. All of her muscles were stiff and she could barely move.

"I should have charged Vincent extra for all the running I had to do. Plus I wore out a new pair of Reeboks."

"What are you going to do?" I asked.

"Take aspirin and get in a hot tub."

Chief Moses called in from Incline, Nevada, on the north shore of Lake Tahoe. Nothing new there yet.

I tried information for Arden Booth but no luck. Theater people tend to be night people so I waited until eleven thirty before I set out by cable car to the Nob Hill address. I got off a few blocks away when I spotted a Chinese restaurant. I ordered a half-dozen Imperial egg rolls to go. A P.I. bearing lunch is a lot more welcome than one that only wants to ask irritating questions.

I walked up the hill with my bag of food to a circa 1920 building that had been renovated and turned into condos. I found Arden's place by going around on a path through a garden behind the building. The garden itself was thick and wild with wisteria and piles of dark green ivy that belonged on an English estate. It was like going through a maze. And it was very private.

I knocked on the heavy wooden door and waited. Then knocked again. The door opened the length of the chain.

Arden's face was up against the crack. "Oh it's you. I couldn't tell for sure through the peephole." Then she yawned.

It's nice to be remembered. She shut the door and undid the chain. Then she let me in without even asking what I wanted.

Our other interview had been brief. Now I had a little more to go on.

Arden Booth was fragile looking. She wasn't much taller than five feet two and she couldn't have weighed much more than a hundred pounds soaking wet. She wore her dark brown hair cut very short and parted on the side. Her face was small with large brown eyes that gave her a gamin look. She was wearing a shimmering pink sweat suit and pink and white aerobic shoes. If I were into clichés I would say she was as cute as a belly button.

An early morning exercise show was on TV. Obviously taped earlier by Arden.

"What do you want now?" she asked. "I told you everything I knew."

"I just wanted to bring you some lunch."

I handed her the bag of Imperial egg rolls. When she opened it she smiled and those large eyes widened even more. She sat down on the bare floor and took a bite. "Hot," she said and offered me one.

I shook my head. She could use all the food she could get.

While she ate I looked around the room. There wasn't much to see. Everything was packed up in cartons.

"Just moving in?" I asked as I wondered how she could afford the place.

"No," she said between bites. She was halfway through the second eggroll with no sign of a slowdown. "Moving out. I can't afford the rent."

"I'm not surprised. But I heard you just moved in."

"So?"

"This is not a motel you're moving in and out of."

According to St. John

I let her think it over while she devoured the third egg roll. "Something changed in my personal life. That's all. Something just didn't work out."

"It happens," I said.

"Damn right."

After the third one she took a break. And yawned again.

"Care to tell me about it?"

"No. It's personal."

"I hear you were very upset by Amanda Cole's death."

Arden rolled up the top of the egg roll bag. "Yes. Anything wrong with that?"

"She didn't have many friends."

"Well I was one of them. She was always nice to me. She even helped me get the part of Lady Macduff."

"Then you knew her before."

"I had a stick part in a play with her last year."

"Stick?"

"Yeah. You stand there like a stick in the mud and don't say a damn thing."

"So you got along well with her."

"Yes."

"That was unusual."

"She wasn't the bitch everyone made her out to be."

"Would you say you were close?"

"Yes. I guess so."

"Did she ever confide in you?"

She shifted uncomfortably. She reopened the bag and took out the fourth egg roll. She offered me one again. This time I accepted. "Sometimes."

"Was she faithful to her husband? Was she having an affair?"

I ate my egg roll and watched her eyes. They were avoiding mine. She knew something.

She took out the last egg roll and held it in her hand. "I shouldn't tell you," she said.

"The woman is dead."

"So?"

"I'll keep it confidential if I can. Only if it's essential to Denny's case."

"She took a bite and said, "I'm full."

I wasn't surprised.

"She was having an affair with Julian Kismodel."

I wasn't surprised.

But that was only the half of it.

From Arden's apartment I went to Forsander and Samaho's office.

The three of us sat down in the conference room. I smelled liniment and rubbing alcohol. They were both aching from a rough basketball game the night before.

"This is getting too tough," Brian complained. "We're almost out of subs. Scott and I are too old to play the whole game."

"At least it keeps you away from unsafe sex."

They talked about getting me to play during the last weeks of the season.

"Before we die out on the court," Scott said.

I got up and stretched my back. "Let me think about it. Remember I'm not on the roster. You could forfeit the game if anyone on the other team found out."

They both just grinned.

With basketball out of the way, I went over the investigation from Leo Stubbs to Arden's revelation of Amanda's affair with Kismodel.

"Who do you like?" he asked.

"We have a cuckold," I said. "Parker Rinshell has to be a suspect. And he was backstage in Amanda's dressing room."

"We need something solid," Brian said as he rubbed the back of his neck.

Scott stretched his leg out and started to massage the back of his thigh. "Hamstring pull," he said.

"Why don't you guys take two aspirin and go see the trainer in the morning?"

They let that go by.

"What we do need is a break before the Preliminary Hearing. We don't want Denny bound over for trial if we can avoid it."

"So what do you want?"

"We want you to stop sitting around here talking hoops when you should be out busting your ass to break this one open."

According to St. John

I got up. "Don't bother to stand. I can see it's next to impossible."

They didn't.

"Just a reminder while I bust my ass. The agency hasn't been paid yet."

"Neither have we," Brian said.

"But you're getting great coverage in the newspapers for this one. You guys are getting famous in the city for the Lady Macbeth case."

"That's only fair," Scott said and then groaned as he tried to move his leg.

"Try a Bike thigh cap wrap," I advised. "It'll help the hamstring."

I left before Scott could express his appreciation.

That night, exactly two weeks after Amanda Cole's death, I was watching one of my favorite movies: *Bullitt* with Steve McQueen as a San Francisco police detective with the ornery instincts of a good P.I. Besides McQueen there was Jacqueline Bisset to watch and some of the greatest car chase sequences ever filmed. And all on location in the city. When Frank Bullitt took a turn in his old green Mustang at an impossible speed, I wished I could drive like that and not end up in jail or more likely in the morgue.

As he cut off a cable car the phone rang. "Shit," I muttered.

It was Johnny D. "Jeremiah, I'm callin' from the theater. I only got a few minutes but you gotta promise me you won't come rushin' down here."

I turned down the TV. "Why should I?"

" 'Cause Eric Ullwanger's dead."

"How?"

"We're investigatin' but it looks like a definite suicide. We got a note an' other evidence."

"How'd he do it?"

"Hung himself in his dressing room with a noose from the prop room. Real handy."

"What did the note say?"

"For P.R., I can't take it. Eric."

"That it?"

"Yeah."

"What about the other evidence?"

"We found a couple of medical reports with his personal effects. There's the result of an Elissa test—positive for HIV. And a later confirming report from a Western Blot test. The man had just been diagnosed with AIDS."

"How did he get these reports? Did they just come in the mail?"

"Yeah. That's it."

"That's crazy. No counseling. No nothing. Just a death notice delivered by the mailman."

"It's from a private for-profit clinic. That's how the pricks operate."

"Keeps costs down," I said.

"Yeah."

"What's the date on the second report? The Western Blot?" This test was far more accurate than the Elissa. It would confirm the AIDS diagnosis.

"I gotta go!"

"The date or I'm coming down there to get your ass in a sling with Chang."

"All right. All right. It's in an envelope postmarked October 9. That mean anything?"

"I don't know."

"Don't hold out on me, St. John."

"I don't know." P.I.'s have to hold out.

"Whaddya you make of this P.R. shit?" Johnny asked.

"Obviously a man deeply concerned about his public relations image."

"So he goes and fuckin' hangs himself? That doesn't make sense."

"Suicide hardly ever does."

"Don't know about that. I get this kinda notice about AIDS and I'd eat my gun."

"You have a point, Johnny."

"Okay? You got enough? You're not comin' down here are you?"

"I think you gave me everything I could get." I hung up. I wanted to see the suicide scene myself but I knew Chang would make it hard as hell and Johnny D. would be rightfully pissed off if I showed up after all he had given me. So I turned up the TV

According to St. John

sound. The chase was still on. I watched it while I considered the note and the evidence.

The postmark date was significant. If the report had been mailed October 9, a Friday it wouldn't have reached Ullwanger because of the weekend and the Columbus Day holiday until the 13th. The night of the opening. The night when he seemed so depressed. The night he got drunk with us. It was also the night Parker Rinshell went to see Eric before he went to see his sick wife. Because he knew Eric was a hell of a lot sicker? And as for P.R., public relations like hell, the message was directed to Parker Rinshell. All of this was making some sense. And then I stirred in the affair that Amanda was apparently having with Kismodel. And I had . . . I wasn't sure what I had but everything was moving the evidence away from Denny and into a lot of kinky bedrooms.

The movie was over. I knew it was late but I called Mickey to see how she was and to discuss what I had learned.

She was resting in bed with a heating pad and a glass of wine. She was feeling like she could move again. But for now she was content to listen to me.

"Good work. And good night, Jeremiah," she said when I finished.

"Don't you miss me at times like these?"

"Times like what?"

"Bedtimes."

"I'm taking the Fifth."

"Gin or vodka?"

She hung up. But at least she didn't slam the phone down.

18

First thing Wednesday morning Leo Stubbs showed up. Leo was happy to learn how good Kismodel was looking as a suspect.
"Next it's Maydik, Jerry."
I winced.
"I'll see what I can do. This is still ass backwards."
"Who gives a fuck?"
As Leo left, the Chief arrived after driving in the early morning hours from Tahoe. I barely got Leo by Chief Moses without a confrontation. He still resented the intrusion into our office space.
"Our sacred ground," he called it.
I wasn't sure what he meant and didn't push to find out.
I told him what I had told Mickey last night. When she arrived, feeling in much less pain, we all decided to descend on Parker Rinshell. Parker had been nice enough to tell us about the commercial he was shooting this week along the Great Ocean Highway at a Professional Surfing Tour stop.

We drove the highway in the T-Bird with the windows open. The salt was tangible in air thick with moisture from the sea. No one complained about the seats this cloudless morning.

The waves looked high, pipelines that belonged more in Hawaii than in Northern California.

We continued along. To our right there was a broad parking area with few cars, then a concrete wall, then a stretch of wet sand beach. The surf was pounding and few people were in the water. The few cars in the parking lots were topped by one or, more frequently, a pair of surfboards. Anyone surfing in these waters would be wearing a wet suit. We proceeded south, past the windmill at the western edge of Golden Gate Park. Ahead of us one of the parking lots was full. We pulled into it anyway. A huge banner announcing the PST competition was stretched out over the side of a trailer. If they raised it any higher it would flap violently in the ocean wind.

There were about fifteen trailers and another dozen RV's squatting on the lot. The rest of the spaces belonged mostly to spectators. I drove over to the next lot and found a place to park without a problem.

The three of us walked back along the seawall between the parking lot and the beach. Off-shore we could see the surfers, tanned and rugged-looking, catching waves and riding them in. The girls on the beach were dressed to a rear end in French cut bikinis in bright colors and floral prints. They all looked cold. Most of them had thermoses of hot liquid for help against the cold Pacific breeze. None of them would think of covering up.

"It wasn't like this for Balboa," I said.

"Just another white man. The forerunner of the real estate agent," the Chief said as he watched a particularly well-filled bikini pass by.

"Are you complaining?" Mickey asked.

"Not about that. One of the few positive legacies of colonization."

We spotted Parker Rinshell about twenty-five yards down from us by the seawall. The area was roped off for Parker's filming. He was dressed in long garishly printed surfer trunks and was pitching a detergent that had some tenuous connection to churning and foaming surf—the kind of action that got the dirt out. Cute idea for

According to St. John

the housewives of America. I imagined what the sponsors wanted were shots of hunks on surf boards to titillate their customers. Parker, who was wearing his blond wig, was only the talking head.

Parker could have studied those lines a little better. We waited impatiently through five takes until he got it right.

"Okay. That's a wrap. We'll cut in the surfer closeups later," the director announced. He looked to be about seventeen years old. Probably the boy wonder of commercial making. Or with a father high up in the company. Either way I had to admit he seemed to know what he was doing.

We followed Parker to his trailer and got to him before he could get into it.

"Remember us?" I said.

"Two of you. I see you brought along a muscular friend."

I introduced Chief Moses. I wanted everything done professionally. "He's a consultant," I said.

"I don't doubt it."

Parker wrapped his arms around his thin chest. "I'm freezing. Let me get into the trailer."

The Chief just happened to be blocking his way.

"Not without us," I said.

"I talked to you already, St. Whatever."

"John," I said. "But that was Sunday. This is Wednesday. There are always new and exciting things to talk about."

"All right."

The Chief let him by and he unlocked the trailer door. We followed him inside.

It was cramped in the small trailer. We found places to sit on cushions on the fold-down benches that ran along each wall while Parker opened a wardrobe and pulled on a chartreuse jogging suit in a velour material. The kind of suit I would object to being buried in. But on him it looked appropriate if not good. There was a small electric heater and he turned it on. The coils glowed red and immediately it started radiating heat.

When we were all seated and reasonably comfortable—if four adults could be comfortable in an oversized closet—I said, "Your wife was having an affair. That gives you a motive for murder."

"Not much for small talk, are you?"

"Not today."

Parker rubbed his hands together. "Of course she was having an affair. But that didn't give me a motive. It never did."

I looked at Mickey and the Chief. The Chief nodded. It was clear to all of us.

"You know about Eric Ullwanger?" I asked.

"Of course."

"Lots of opportunities for advancement in this company," Chief Moses said. "The way the major players are departing."

"He wrote his suicide note to you. P.R. Parker Rinshell."

Parker got up. He walked around in the trailer. He didn't get far. "You can't prove that."

"You were Ullwanger's lover," I said.

"I wonder what the lady thought of that," the Chief muttered. He was not keen on what he saw as unnatural acts either with men or alligators.

Parker Rinshell laughed. "The lady—if you mean my wife—thought nothing. Ours was a marriage of convenience. To hide my sexual preference when it seemed wise to do so. At times, in the seventies, I almost came out of the closet. But we were used to each other; we had the kind of sex lives we wanted and an asexual security. And then AIDS hit the gay community. I couldn't come out. I would have been stigmatized. Gays were briefly in. Now they are out. You can't get an actor to play a realistic gay part. They get identified with it and it's box office suicide."

"So each of you went your separate ways?" Mickey said.

"More or less. We never had sex together our entire marriage. Which turned out just fine for Amanda. You see I've tested positive for the HIV virus. It's probably only a matter of time. Like Ullwanger."

"Do you know who she was having an affair with?" I asked.

He went over to a suitcase and took out an audio tape. "I found this in her room."

"What is it?" I asked.

"The sounds of her and Julian Kismodel at play."

He tossed it to me. "Keep it. It may help you. I certainly don't want it."

"Either they were using it for erotic stimulation or . . ." Mickey began.

According to St. John

"Could be better than the Venus Butterfly stroke," I said.

"Or she was using it for blackmail," the Chief concluded.

"That's why I brought these two along," I said. "Brain power."

"If Julian Kismodel's wife heard that tape she'd cut him off without a cent," Parker said as he sat down on the one chair in the trailer. It was getting warm in the confined space and he turned down the electric heater.

"You've been illuminating so far," I said. "Now would you look at these keys. They were Amanda's."

"Should you have them?"

"The police sometimes need help," the Chief said.

Parker took the keys. "Her car keys. And her house key. This one. Those are the only ones I recognize." He took out his keys and matched his house key to hers. That left us with two mysterious keys. And one mysterious key reappearance—the fire door to the theater.

"Did she live with you in Sausalito?" I asked.

"Of course."

"She didn't spend nights away?"

He got up and looked at a window splattered with salt water. The sea and the surf were barely visible through the gray veil.

"I cared for her in my own way. And she cared for me. We spent a lot of time together, but yes we spent a lot of nights apart."

"Did she have another place in the city?"

"I don't know. Nothing she owned. I didn't find anything concerning property or the like after her death."

"But she had a place to go."

"Just try those keys all over the city. See what you come up with."

Not a bad idea. Too bad it was a little impractical.

On the drive back we had a lot to consider.

"The tape is a big item," the Chief said.

"The big motive," Mickey said.

Kismodel was looking better and better.

"He is going to want his tape. He is not going to want to lose his squaw's money and get sent back broke to the reservation."

"But he doesn't know who has it," I said.

"There are no secrets among enemies," the Chief noted.

"When are you going to bring some of this to Johnny D. and Chang?" Mickey asked.

"When we have something firm. And after I consult with Denny's attorneys of record."

I turned off the Great Ocean Highway by Seal Rock and the Cliff House Restaurant. The sun had moved overhead and was firing the lines of waves now far below us with sparks. Two blocks inland and it was almost warm.

Back at the office I called Forsander and Samaho and after a stint with the Boss on hold I got to Scott.

"No comment on the music?" he asked.

"Next time try Kiss."

"Sure. Stick out your lips."

"Not these days, lover boy."

I asked him to check Amanda Cole's autopsy report for the HIV virus.

"Why?"

"Morbid curiosity."

"Come on."

"I've got a bet with Mickey."

Scott muttered a curse and put me back on hold. I listened to the Boss sing about his hometown.

Scott came back on the line. "The HIV test was negative."

Chances were that Parker was telling the truth. Amanda had avoided infection by not having sex with her gay husband. But she didn't avoid death through other sexual practices—whatever they might turn out to be. I told everything I had learned to Scott.

"Things are looking better for Denny," he said.

"That's what you're paying me for."

"One thing," Scott said.

"About paying me?"

"Yes. Don't move too fast on Kismodel. He still owes us some big bucks and I don't think he'll be inclined to pay if we get Denny off by fingering him for the cops."

"It's going to be touch and go," I said.

"No. It's going to be grab the money and run."

"Spoken like a true member of the bar," I said as I hung up.

According to St. John

I went out into the front office and told Mickey to bill Forsander and Samaho for our services rendered.

"We want Kismodel to pay before the roof falls in on him."

Mickey smiled and got out an invoice. The telephone rang. It was Leo Stubbs wanting an update. I went back into my office to take the call. Against my better judgment I told him what we had learned.

I could tell he was dancing on his desk.

19

That Friday the Chief got the call he was waiting for and left for Tahoe.

I met with Carrie and told her I was getting out of high-risk investing.

"I told you. I have a no-risk investment plan." She looked at me through those oversized glasses.

"Tell me about it," I said.

"Not here. Over lunch."

Carrie took me to a place called The Taxi Cab. It was a crowded and noisy place the size of a raquetball court with about as much decor. The menu offered French and Japanese dishes. I ordered a Henry's and something Japanese that was cooked. Carrie ordered a vodka gimlet and a snail and mushroom omelet. Must be part of the image. We had to lean over the small table to hear each other.

She proposed a deal that would guarantee a profit for me and for her in futures. The plan was simple. It merely involved defrauding the brokerage house. Carrie would monitor the house's investments in the Standard and Poor's 500-stock index futures and divert the profitable transactions to my personal account. Any losses I took would likewise be diverted to the brokerage house account. Simple. Elegant. Just like Carrie.

"I have a number of other clients in the program with me already," she explained over a second vodka gimlet.

"What do I have to do?"

"Since there is no risk, you simply divide the profits with me"

She went into greater detail. Over a fruit dessert I bought into her investment plan.

The only problem for Carrie besides picking up the check was the wire I was wearing. Mickey followed us in a rented van after we left the brokerage house. From where we sat I could see it. She was getting it all on tape.

Carrie went back to the office and I went back to check on the quality of the tape. I was concerned about all the noise in the restaurant, but it had come out fine.

We drove back to Carrie's office and I had Mickey, who was unknown in the place, deliver the tape to the man in charge.

He could handle Carrie as he saw fit. But one thing was certain. Her broker days were over.

I got a call late in the afternoon from Leo Stubbs. He had a meeting set up with the Marina Theater Candy Man and he wanted me along. I agreed. I decided to bring Mickey along for moral support.

We were to meet at a Potrero Hill bar. The Potrero district combines industrial warehouses, artists' studios, and wholesale furnishings outlets, bringing together blue collar workers, Bohemians, interior decorators, and various other professionals who found the area attractive. The most desirable section was the Hill itself with its views of the eastern waterfront and its location in the city's narrow summer sunshine belt.

It is rumored that the best outdoor basketball in the city is played in its school playgrounds.

The address Leo gave me was out of cable car range but it was usually not impossible to find a parking space after five. I drove over and found one on a steep side street. It was a narrow spot be-

According to St. John

tween two driveways and the T-Bird just made it. I turned the wheels into the curb to prevent the car from rolling downhill. You could also be ticketed if you didn't.

The bar was on the corner and was called appropriately enough the Corner Bar. Creativity lives in the Potrero. Leo Stubbs was standing outside in his belted trench coat smoking a cigarette in front on the neon Coors sign in the window. He opened the door and we went in.

This was not one of the upscale bars in the neighborhood but one that got its customers from the warehouse workers. The bar decor was every beer promo poster printed in the last twenty years. There was a scarred wooden bar, leatherette bar stools, tables, chairs, two booths in the back and a large pool table under a yellow circle of light. There was an old TV over the bar but it wasn't on. I suspected it didn't work. No big-screen Monday night football parties for the Corner Bar.

The barstools were almost all taken. Half the tables were filled. Two men moved around the green felt of the pool table, playing eight ball. Their bottles of Bud were balanced on each side of the table. I watched one of the players, a small wiry man in a blue T-shirt chalk up his cue furiously.

"Come on, asshole, I ain't got all fuckin' day," his much younger opponent said.

"You want this pool cue up your ass, kid?"

Apparently not. The kid stopped rushing the man and drank some beer instead.

We moved to one of the two booths in the back. Every head turned as Mickey passed. Except for a heavyset blonde helping behind the bar she was the only woman in the place.

"They keep these open for certain business transactions," Leo said.

Mickey nodded. "Like dope and bookmaking."

Leo smiled. "The lady knows her stuff."

"I used to be a cop."

Leo stopped smiling. "Oh." Leo hadn't done all of his homework.

I ordered a Henry's and Mickey ordered a Foster's Australian lager.

"Switching from wine?" I asked.

"I'd rather have a sealed bottle in this place. Besides I think Paul Hogan's cute. I love his accent."

Leo ordered a bottled wine cooler. The man must have destroyed his taste buds smoking.

Leo crushed out his cigarette in a cheap tin ashtray. We concentrated on watching the door.

When Leo lit up again, I said, "This is the no smoking booth."

"Fuck you, Jerry."

I barely resisted my impulse to put out the cigarette in his face.

Exactly one cigarette later the door to the place opened up and a young Hispanic male came in. He said something like "Yo" to everyone in the bar. He had thick black hair, a dark handsome face, a shirt unbuttoned to the navel, and crotch-hugging black pants that were tucked into lizard cowboy boots. If I were in his line of business I would have worn Nikes. But maybe he had a horse tied up outside. The horse would have to handle about twenty pounds of gold chain—what our man was wearing around his neck—besides the rider.

He stepped up to our booth and opened up a huge grin that revealed one gold tooth and a lot of stained enamel. He was staring at Mickey.

"Eyes to yourself, asshole," she said.

The smirk disappeared. "Don't you talk to me like that, beetch," He was leaning forward, threatening.

Before he could do anything I had him by his convenient chains. "Shut up, punk, and sit down," I said as I twisted them into his neck.

"Leggo, man."

"You going to behave with the lady?"

"You say so."

"I say so."

"We gotta get off to a better start here, boys," Leo interjected.

"You say so." I pulled the Candy Man into the booth and let go of the gold leash.

He started rubbing his neck and cursing softly in rapid Spanish.

"You coulda hurt me, man."

Mickey looked at him. "Get macho," she said.

According to St. John

The Candy Man jerked upright, his hands in front of his chest like he wanted to wring her neck.

"Easy man," I said.

He dropped his hands. He said, "Stubbs, you tol' me we got some business here."

Leo turned to me. "Steban here's the Candy Man for the Marina Theater. He's agreed to answer our questions."

"So?" I asked.

"He ain't workin' for free, St. John."

I wished we had something on the bastard.

"You got a hundred?" Leo asked.

Leo had warned me on the phone that's what it would cost. I pulled out a hundred dollar bill from my wallet.

"This better be worth it, Steban."

"Don' worry, man."

"That Sunday night before the murder, who'd you sell to?" I asked.

"Was a real slow night."

"How slow?" Mickey asked.

"I sell the shit to the good lookin' one with the long black hair. The one that got a man's name. Denny or somethin' like that."

"Anyone else?"

"That black broad. Leah X. she call herself."

Leo was growing impatient. These were not the people on his list. "What about Kismodel and Maydik?"

Steban just shook his head. "They don' do no business with me."

"Shit," Leo said. He pressed Steban on it. It didn't do any good. He named other cast members who bought from time to time but not the two Leo wanted.

"What about Amanda Cole."

"I don't speak ill a the dead. 'Sides she never was no customer."

"Could they have been buying from someone else?" I asked.

"No way. Not in my territory."

"Outside of it?" Mickey asked.

"This a big city, lady." Steban got up and swaggered his way to the bar. He was regaining his poise or whatever he called it.

"Shit," Leo said. "We didn't tie the coke up with Kismodel and Maydik."

179

"I'm not so sure about that," Mickey said.
"You got an idea?" he asked.
She was a step ahead of me.
"Leah X.," she said as she finished her Foster's from the bottle. She didn't even want to use one of the glasses from this place.
"She ain't who we're after," Leo complained.
"Conspiracy, Leo, conspiracy. Leah is in love with Maydik. She poisons Amanda not out of jealousy but to get Maydik his payday," Mickey explained.
"I love it. Now I know who got the brains in your operation, St. John."
"Who?" I asked.
Mickey brushed a wave of blond hair from her forehead and smiled at me. The memories of us together suddenly washed over me.

It was early enough to go to the theater and confront Leah. The two of us and Leo. What a team.
We found her backstage talking to Arden Booth.
"We need to talk to Leah in private," I said to Arden.
She nodded and disappeared into a dressing room.
"You don't have to go anywhere," Leah said, but it was too late.
Leah looked stunning tonight. Her ebony skin was beautifully made up and her cropped hairdo looked perfect set off by an elegant amber and silver necklace and matching earrings. She was wearing a black jersey dress with a tank top that revealed her voluptuous figure. She had on sexy black strip sandals with spike heels that added to her already impressive height.
"Fuck off, honkies," she said. This was going to be even more difficult than I thought.
I grabbed her arm and squeezed just hard enough to let her know I meant business. "We have a man named Steban to talk about, Leah."
She struggled to free her arm.
"Don't know any Steban."
Leo decided it was his turn to come on. "Says he's been sellin' you coke. Says he sold you some just before Amanda got her fatal dose. Whaddya think about that?"

According to St. John

"You saying I poisoned that bitch?"

"You could have wanted to help Maydik to the insurance money," Mickey said.

"Say what? What are you talking about?" She looked genuinely puzzled. It was likely that she didn't know. Pressing it didn't get us anything more.

"What about jealousy? The rumor that Maydik was making it with Amanda Cole," I tried.

"You got the wrong rumor, man."

I wasn't sure where to go next when Mickey interjected, "What was the right rumor?"

I expected to hear about Kismodel.

"Amanda, she comes from the Isle of Lesbo."

"What?" I said.

"She's a lesbian."

"She's had affairs with men," I said.

"Don't be naive. She used them. When they got used up she dropped them like an old lipstick. The woman liked the ladies."

"You have any evidence?" Mickey asked.

"Sure. Personal experience. She come on to me."

"And?" Leo asked.

"I try anything. Once."

I dropped Leo off at his office building in a seedy part of the city south of Market, and drove Mickey home.

"Parker Rinshell left out just one little item about his wife," she said as we got to her building.

"I wonder why. He came across with everything else."

"Or so he wanted us to believe."

I shrugged. I tended to believe there was one secret about Amanda that Parker wanted to keep to himself. "We're getting closer," I said. "I think I see a pattern and the two keys could be the answer."

"You just have to find the right doors to open."

"I've got at least one idea. If it works out it could lead us to the last door."

"Dreamer," she said.

"You know I am. Enough of one to invite myself up tonight."

For the first time in a while she was considering one of my offers seriously. She leaned over the stick shift and kissed me hard on the lips. I took that as a yes.

Unfortunately she meant it as a goodnight kiss. That was where she left it.

"Give me a little space, Jeremiah," she said as she got out of the car.

"Take all you need," I said, annoyed. I waited until the lights went on in her apartment to make sure she was safe.

Back upstairs in my rooms I drank a Henry's and although it was very late I called Denny to apologize for our last time together. I told her what I had learned about Kismodel and everyone else.

She invited us all to the annual Halloween masquerade party put on by the Actors' Guild at the Palace of Fine Arts.

"Who'll be there from the theater company?"

"Everyone."

"I accept for the agency but the Chief is out of town."

"Too bad."

She invited me over to her place.

"No expectations," she said.

I didn't believe her but I went anyway.

20

Denny had expectations. Only lowered. She proposed no-risk sexual practices which turned out to be pretty damn good.

"You take what you can get," she said as she rolled naked out of bed.

"You should put all of this down and sell it to *Cosmo* or *Ms.*," I suggested.

"No way I'm sharing," she said.

"I understand your point."

She rolled back into bed. We performed a safe-sex variation of the Venus Butterfly at Denny's request. Again.

Then she put on her latex gloves and took me in hand. Again.

On Saturday morning I woke up to Mickey's typing downstairs. I covered my ears with a pillow but that didn't work. I hoped a computer would be quieter than her old electric machine. I gave up trying to sleep and got up to take a shower.

When I came down I asked, "What are you doing here?"
"Some catching up."
"It's damn noisy."
"Rough night, sweetie?" She smiled.
"Interesting at least."
I left her to the catching up and went out and got a cable car. Twenty minutes later I was about to test out my theory on one of the mystery keys. After making sure no one was in I tried one of the two keys. It unlocked the door and the deadbolt above it.

I slipped through the living room and into the bedroom and opened the closet. I found what I hoped I would find. A costume. This one was a Rudolph Valentino, complete with a larger than life full-face mask.

I shut the closet door, made my way through the cluttered rooms, and locked the front door.

There was one more key to go.

"We're going to the Actors' Guild Masquerade Ball tonight," I announced to Mickey when I returned.

"I don't have a thing to wear."

"There's a costume shop a few blocks from here. Let's lock up and see what we come up with."

"It's Halloween. There won't be anything left."

We walked the two blocks to the costume shop. Mickey was right. The proprietor, dressed in a Dracula costume and mask himself, showed us what little he had left.

"You should have come sooner," he said in what he thought was a Transylvanian accent.

"Next year, we'll shop early."

"Everybody in the city loves to dress up."

Halloween was a kind of city holiday in the pre-AIDS days when gays got to dress up in whatever queen clothes they wanted to and parade around. It was still a big day in the Castro but a lot of the joy had gone out of the celebration. In fact, the straights seemed to be recapturing the holiday these days. And so were even a few kids.

Dracula rolled out a single rack of costumes.

"What about this bunch of grapes for the lady?" he asked.

"What is it?" Mickey asked.

"Purple balloons strung together."

According to St. John

"What happens when they pop?"

He shrugged. "Most women wear a flesh-colored leotard under the balloons. But it's not necessary."

"Is that a Wonder Woman?"

"I forgot about that one. A man returned it today. He said he wouldn't let his wife wear it. He exchanged it for a Bo Peep costume. Updated with garter belt and G-string."

"Weirdo," Mickey said.

"At least this is Halloween. You should see what the people want who come in here during the off season."

"I'd rather not," I said.

"I'll take Wonder Woman," Mickey said.

"And you, sir?"

Almost all of the costumes were for women.

"Here's a Marie Antoinette," Mickey suggested.

"This flapper dress was very popular," Dracula said.

I turned away from the costumes and said, "I'll take what you have on."

"Wait sir, this one is not for rent. I need it for tonight myself."

I tugged off the mask. The face beneath it was young and heavily made up.

"Look at all these wonderful costumes," I said. "Here you can be Daisy Duck. Or Alice. How much for the Dracula suit?"

He quoted a ridiculous figure.

I came back with a lower one that was still high enough for him not to refuse.

"You have a deal," he said in Transylvanian as he removed his red satin-lined black cape. "A stake for your heart is included."

"And silver bullets?"

"All out. But the stake works just as well."

"I'll remember that," I said.

I picked Mickey up at her apartment for the ball. She looked like the perfect Wonder Woman.

"Nice costume," I said as she tried to pull the top up to cover a little more of her breasts.

"The damn thing's cut so low."

"I like it."

"You would."

We drove to the Palace of Fine Arts. The building was awash in light. It had been built in 1915 for the Pan Pacific Exposition and restored in 1958. The temple was meant to look like a Roman ruin and it did. It also looked like it had been put together from pieces of the Jefferson and Lincoln Memorials in D.C. During the day its color is sandstone. Tonight the lights flooding it were pink. Someone's idea of a Halloween color.

We parked on Bay Street only five blocks away and put on our masks.

As we walked to the main entrance arch I explained to Mickey what I wanted her to do. She didn't like it.

"Why didn't you tell me about this before?"

"You might not have gone along with it."

"I don't like it!"

"You don't have to like it. Just do it!"

Mickey stamped the Wonder Woman boots she wore on her own great Wonder Woman legs but didn't say anything else.

You're dressed perfectly for it," I said.

"You tricked me," she complained one last time. She would be ready for business now.

We used Denny's name to get in. The ruined temple was decorated inside with orange and black crepe paper, carved pumpkins, monsters, witches, and things that looked like real human skeletons. There was a bandstand set up and on it sat a five-piece group all in Raggedy Ann and Andy costumes. Cute. The center space was the dance floor and the musicians were playing ballroom music. There were couples out on the floor. Because of the costumes there were some pretty unusual pairings. Occasionally the pink light from outside swept through the building. It was eerie.

There was a bar set up under one of the temple arches. Drinks were going for five bucks a shot. I bought Mickey a glass of white wine and myself a bottle of Moosehead, the only beer they had. We had to lift the masks above our mouths to drink.

I sent Mickey in search of Rudolph Valentino. As for me I went hunting for Cleopatra—the costume Denny told me she would be wearing.

I found Cleopatra and came up behind her and tried to bite her neck. It was hard to do with the mask on. That turned out to be a good thing because this Cleopatra turned out to be someone other

According to St. John

than Denny. I thought they only allowed one of a kind at these balls. Obviously not, as I spotted two other Draculas. What happened to costume creativity?

I snuck up behind another masked Cleopatra. She was getting a drink at the bar. This time I whispered "Denny?" in her ear.

"Bite me and find out."

It was Denny. She finished her gimlet and we danced a jitterbug and then did a very sexy tango. I looked around the room. Wonder Woman was dancing with Rudolph Valentino. Even through Valentino was wearing lifts Mickey still towered over him. But they moved well together. I steered Denny over towards them.

"Recognize that couple?" I asked.

"That's Mickey with the Wonder Woman mask," she said.

"And her partner?"

"I don't know."

"It's a good costume." I wouldn't have known either except for my visit to the apartment earlier today.

After the next dance I saw Mickey and Valentino go out into the gardens by the pond. I had nothing to do now but wait. And dance with Denny.

Twenty minutes later I was in the middle of a slow dance with Denny when Mickey tapped her shoulder and cut in.

"My God! Pursued by such awesome women," I said.

Denny bowed out gracefully.

"Stick it, Jeremiah," Mickey said. "That was not fun."

"Tell me about it anyway."

"You were right about Valentino." She gave me a quick rundown.

"Where is old Rudolph?"

"Waiting for me on a bench by the pond while I get a drink. We have some plans for the evening to discuss."

I went out of the palace building, past some contrived ruins, to the pool of water. The pink lights glimmered through the bushes and trees. The night was clear but cool. Rudolph was waiting on a bench.

I sat down next to Valentino.

"That's taken. I'm waiting for someone." The voice was straining for a baritone but came out tenor.

"Wonder Woman isn't coming back."

"Who are you?"

"Count Dracula." I flashed the black cape across my mask. Valentino started to get up.

"Sit down." I tugged at his costume sleeve.

"Let go."

"I can sell you a stake to drive into my heart." But I didn't let go. Rudolph sat.

"I'm not really Count Dracula. I'm Jeremiah St. John." I pulled up my mask.

Silence.

"Wonder Woman is my partner."

"I should have known. She tell you everything?"

"No. She told me you came on to her. Invited her back to your place. I don't care about that. There are other things I want to hear about."

"Like what?"

"Like about you and Amanda Cole?"

A hand came up and pulled off the Valentino disguise. Underneath the mask was the face of Arden Booth. She stared blankly at me.

"One of the keys on Amanda's key ring was for your condo."

Arden stood up. In her dark suit she looked fragile. Moonlight splashed on the pond water. I was afraid she was going to try to run away. Instead she said, "She was in love with me."

"Did she set you up in that Nob Hill apartment."

"Yes. That's why I have to move out. I don't have the rent."

"This affair between you two was recent?"

"Very. We were going to start a new life together."

"You mean she was leaving her husband?"

"Of course not. We would be together when we could. That's all."

"What about Kismodel?"

"What about him? He's a man. She used him. She used him up. That's all."

"Then there is a large question here. If she was setting up this love nest with you, was she leaving another woman?"

Arden moved across into the shadows. "I don't know."

"Are you sure?" I got up to follow her.

According to St. John

"All right. She was leaving someone she's been with a long time. She felt bad about it but she loved me."

"Who was this woman?"

"She would never tell me."

"Why not?"

"She said she could never tell anyone."

I took out Amanda's keys and looked at them. One more door to unlock. Maybe.

I left Arden alone by the water. I could hear her beginning to cry as I walked away.

Back inside I told Mickey about Amanda's last lover.

Mickey said, "If you suggest I flirt with another woman I'll kick you in your Dracula balls."

"I think I'll go dance with Denny."

After dropping off Mickey and Denny I went back home alone. It was very late or very early.

I opened the door to a surprise. Halloween was not over.

On the steps above me stood a facsimile of Rambo. Rambo had thick black hair, black greasepaint on his face and hands, and a brown and green camouflage costume complete with an M-16 that looked real.

"Trick or treat," he said.

"I'll take the treat."

"Oh yeah? You a wise ass?"

"It's possible. I've been called that. And worse."

He came down the steps and nudged me back into my office with the barrel of the submachine gun.

"Like your costume," I said.

"Can't say the same for you."

I had taken off the mask and the cape. There wasn't much of a costume left.

"That a toy gun?" I asked as I sat down on the couch in my office.

He turned and fired several rounds that ripped into my door.

"They make such realistic toys these days," I said. "Even like real bullets."

"Listen asshole, I didn't come here for small talk."

"That's all I have to offer. I'm all out of candy."

"I come here for the tape!"

"What tape?"

"Mr. Kismodel's tape."

"I didn't know he had one."

"Cut the bullshit." He fired another blast at the door. "You wanna be next?"

No. I didn't want to be. I came up with the tape.

"You would have found it if you tossed the office," I said.

"A lot more fuckin' fun this way. And now get offa Mr. Kismodel's case," Rambo shouted as he went out through the outer offices.

"And a Happy Halloween to you too," I called after him. "Don't take unwrapped candy from strangers."

Everybody was right. I had to do something about security in this place. I looked at my door. Half of it was in splinters. I couldn't leave it like that. It would scare our clients off. I decided to call a carpenter on Monday.

I went upstairs and made myself a double vodka martini. This was no time for a beer. I was pissed at Rinshell for not telling us about his wife's lesbian tendencies and I assumed he had told Kismodel that I had the tape he wanted.

Even though it was late I wanted Leo to share in the good news. Besides why should he be sleeping when I had just been threatened by Rambo. I woke him up to tell him that Julian Kismodel was looking even better as a suspect these days. At first he was annoyed but he came around.

"Now we gotta see 'bout Maydik," he muttered.

"Why?"

"If he ain't involved he's still a beneficiary."

"That's your Goddamn problem. Not mine."

"Where's your hunger for the fuckin' truth, Jerry?" he shouted into the phone. "Gettin' that broad off ain't enough."

"That's what you say."

"Huh?"

"Sweet dreams." I hung up and went to bed.

21

Early Sunday morning I heard someone moving downstairs.

Not again. I pulled on some jeans, got out my S&W .38, and went down the steps slowly, holding the gun out in front of me in a modified two-handed grip, my left hand cupping the bottom of the walnut handle. At the bottom of the stairs I lowered the gun and looked around the open door to the offices. It was only the Chief and a small male companion. The missing Slater kid.

"Thought I would stop by here first to show you what great tracking can do. This is Ryan."

"Pleased to meet you, Ryan." We shook hands.

"Why the gun?" Chief asked.

I pointed to the door. "A little trick or treating last night."

"You should have treated," Chief Moses said.

"I missed Halloween," Ryan said.

"Never again. Next year you can go with me," the Chief said.

"Oh boy!"

"Don't get too excited. Wait until you see the kinds of costumes he wears." I had seen the Chief at one masquerade party. He came dressed as a brick shithouse.

"I told you. That was the only costume left."

"A common problem."

"I'd better get this young brave back to his mama," the Chief said.

"What about breakfast?" I asked.

"We stopped at a McDonald's on the way in."

"And you know what?" the boy said. "They took the Chief's wampum."

Chief Moses put his arm around the kid. Underneath it all Chief had heart.

"Good job," I said.

"A natural talent of my people."

"Come back after you drop the boy off."

"Will do, Jeremiah."

After they left I worked out briefly in my gym, shaved, showered, and put on cotton blend basketball shorts, a Golden State Warriors T-shirt, and my new Air Jordan high tops. As I ate breakfast I kept the gun on the table. I was ready for either the Chief or Rambo.

When I finished I went downstairs and sat in Mickey's chair to get a view of the street from the window that had painted on it ST. JOHN DETECTIVE AGENCY in gold letters. It was the first day in November and for the first time in a while I looked at the plane trees that rose up the incline of the street. Their leaves were turning brown and half had already fallen to the ground. There was no spectacular display of autumn colors in the city. The temperatures never got cold enough to create the necessary physiological changes in the leaves. Instead we had piles of brown leaves waiting for the city street sweepers to suck up. Autumn was here. The next thing would be the rain. We have a very predictable climate—until something goes crazy with *El Nino* every few years and the rains come whenever they wish. I could see the trees and I could see who was coming up to the office door.

The Chief beat out Rambo who I really wasn't expecting anyway.

"We have some things to talk about," he said as he settled into a chair across from me.

According to St. John

"Don't get too comfortable. We can talk later. First I have other plans."

I brought the Chief upstairs to my basketball court and cajoled him until he put on the basketball gear he kept up there. His FSU Seminole basketball uniform. It was an official one that he had traded a football helmet for years ago. And the uniform looked it.

We hadn't played since my injury but I felt I was ready to go one on one with the big man.

"Are you sure you want to do this?" he asked as he stood under the basket.

No I wasn't sure as I looked at his towering frame. But what the hell. "When you fall off a horse you must get right back on."

"You are stealing my Indian lines, Jeremiah."

"Public domain."

"Another white man trick."

"I'll take the ball out," I said.

We were playing best of seven, fifteen baskets a game, no foul shots. We split the first six games and I was feeling no pain. I was ready for the City League. I dropped the last game 15-3. The Chief just out-muscled me with his wide body.

"Good game," the Chief said.

I nodded in agreement. My jump shot was nearly one hundred percent.

I called Mickey and told her to come over for lunch so we could all catch up on what was happening.

The Chief and I each took showers and then I set up things for lunch. I put out roast beef, pickled peppers, Sonoma Jack cheese, Kaiser rolls, hot mustard and horseradish. I had plenty of Henry's, Bud, and white wine.

When Mickey arrived I went over yesterday's events for everybody. I finished with Rambo and the tape of Amanda and Kismodel.

"A definite motive," the Chief said.

Mickey recounted her evening with Valentino-Arden. She could laugh about it now.

"It was like something out of *Victor/Victoria*," she said.

We finished lunch and I tried to reach Julian Kismodel by phone but couldn't. The man was very good at disappearing. I considered invading his office to see if he was really gone. But I decided we could wait. There were a few more things to put together first.

"Do you want to hear how I used my gambling contacts to rescue the Slater boy?" the Chief who had been waiting patiently asked.

"Speak, Moses," we said in unison.

He told us about the casino owner on the north shore of Lake Tahoe who helped him out and how ultimately he had to rescue the boy from a hotel room above a casino on the south shore of the lake where his father and his girlfriend kept him locked up. "They were feeding him Twinkies and letting him watch cable movies all day."

"The woman had switched her obsession from Bingo to KENO. That's how I tracked her down."

"Nice work," Mickey said.

"The mother was overwhelmed. So I did not even lay the bill on her."

"Send it out first thing tomorrow, Mickey."

"Gratitude does not live long in the heart," the Chief said.

"That's what I meant about the bill."

"One other thing of interest."

"Is it important? I want to catch the 49er-Ram game."

"It is important. A familiar name with big gambling debts kept coming up from my contacts."

"Let me guess. Kismodel," I said.

"No. I bet on Perry Maydik," Mickey said.

"How much?"

"Ten bucks," she said.

"You're on." I looked to the Chief.

"Pay the lady."

"Damn, how did you know?" I asked Mickey.

"He has a gambler's look in his eye."

"Women know that kind of thing. It goes with being naturally predatory and suspicious," Chief Moses said.

"Stick it, Chief," Mickey said. "The man spends a lot of time up in Tahoe. I took that as a clue. Which gives us another suspect."

"They'll have to take numbers soon," I said.

"Who do we go after today?" she asked.

"This Sunday is going to be a day of rest. I'm going to watch the football game. Are you two staying?"

"Beats watching *Macbeth* again," the Chief said.

According to St. John

"I'll stay if you refill my glass of wine," Mickey said.

I opened up the refrigerator and got out the wine. I got myself and the Chief another beer. After all, it was five minutes to kickoff.

"Anything for Wonder Woman," I said. "Chief, you should have seen her costume."

Sunday did not turn out to be a complete day of rest. But we brought it on ourselves. After the game we decided that it was a good time to visit Parker Rinshell.

He wasn't happy to see us but he led us into his library. The Chief, who was seeing it for the first time, was almost speechless.

"A lot better than a trailer," he finally managed to say.

"What do you want now?"

"You gave me the tape and then you told Kismodel I had it. Not very good for my health. Or yours."

"In point of fact I never admitted to Kismodel that I had the tape. He was looking for it. No question about that. But he didn't know who had it."

We put on the pressure but couldn't shake his story. Maybe it was the truth but I doubted it.

"Okay," Mickey said. "You left out something about your wife's affairs. That she also had them with women."

"I didn't want questions about that side of her life."

"We understand," Chief Moses said.

"But now we want answers. Who was she having an affair with?"

"I think the woman's name was Arden Booth, claims she was descended from the infamous assassin."

"Before her."

"There was a woman named Rose Smith. I met her once. She was a stupid little thing. I was surprised at Amanda."

"Was she the one Amanda was dropping to set up housekeeping with Arden Booth?"

"I don't know. She had a long affair. I know that. But she stopped talking about Rose Smith years ago."

"Who did she talk about after Rose Smith?" I asked.

"No one else."

"Could it still have been this Rose Smith?" I persisted.

"I imagine it's possible. Amanda was not a promiscuous woman."

195

"Where do we find her?" Mickey asked.

Parker looked blank. "I can't help you there. Rose Smith had some involvement with the theater. I remember that."

"Would she murder for love?" Chief Moses asked.

Parker thought about it. "I doubt it. But who knows what anyone is capable of."

We drove back to the city knowing a little more than we knew before. I also had a few suspicions about some of our principals but for the moment I wanted to keep them to myself.

For now we could concentrate on locating Rose Smith.

22

On Monday morning I got hold of a carpenter. I noticed in the *Chronicle's* "Sporting Green" that the Warriors would be opening the season at home this coming Saturday. I called the Coliseum Arena in Oakland and charged three tickets to my MasterCard.

Then I announced to my two partners, "I've got tickets for us for the Warrior game this Saturday. I want this case wrapped up by then."

"The Great White Father has spoken," the Chief said.

"I'm getting tired of this case," I said.

"Then we'll do it," Mickey called from the reception desk.

"Right on!" I cheered.

I sat down at my desk and tried to concentrate. The door's splintered condition let me see all the way through the office to the front window. The view was an improvement, as I could see Mickey as well as the plane trees outside. However, for privacy it stunk. The carpenter, of course, wasn't coming until the end of the week. Apparently Halloween is a big night for door damage.

I called Forsander and Samaho and this time got an old Beatles tape and then Brian Samaho. Scott had kept him informed.

"Somebody dressed and armed like Rambo threatened me Halloween night. He wanted us off the investigation."

"That's a good sign."

"Maybe for you. But not for me or my door."

"What are you talking about?"

"Rambo demonstrated his firepower on my office door. It looks like the after on a Stallone movie set."

"Call a carpenter."

"They're as scarce as plumbers."

"And hen's teeth. Anything else?"

I reviewed some of our adventures and reminded him about our bill.

"As soon as Kismodel pays us."

"You better collect quick," I said.

"I know." He changed the subject. "We've got some big games coming up in the City League. How are you feeling? We're out of substitutes."

"I tested the back against the Chief. About ninety percent and no pain. But I'm not on the roster."

"Don't worry about it. I'll talk to Scott."

That ended our conversation. The two attorneys seemed as interested in winning the City League as they were in clearing Denny. Well, maybe both were admirable goals.

I called Leo Stubbs and invited him to come over this afternoon. He accepted.

The last person I invited over for the gathering of the clans was Denny. When I called I woke her up but she agreed to come, especially since I promised dinner afterwards.

"Shall I come dressed to go out?" she asked.

That struck me as a bad idea. With Mickey there, I wanted to be discreet.

"It'll be too early. You'll have time to go home and change. To make yourself even more beautiful." Subtle.

By two o'clock everyone was assembled.

I went over everything. "Amanda was sick. Denny went back to

According to St. John

talk to her. Witnesses saw her. Tainted coke was found in Denny's unlocked dressing room. So far we have determined that Kismodel and Rinshell were backstage talking to Amanda. And of course Maydik, who found the body. Then there's Amanda's affair with Arden Booth. I am presuming a previous lover, possibly a Rose Smith, whom we need to find." I held up the key. "I am assuming this is the key to her door. Then there's the Rambo threat Halloween night—presumably from Kismodel."

"Then I don't have to jump bail yet?" Denny asked. She looked sexy in a short gold corduroy jumper and a white blouse. Actually, Denny could look sexy in a butcher's coat.

"Nor live your life in hiding," I said.

"There is much here for Johnny and Chang," the Chief said.

"I'm sure they know a lot of this themselves."

"But a little help wouldn't hurt," Mickey said.

"Still, there's the testimony that Amanda was trying to score some coke just before Denny came in. And the word of the Candy Man that Denny bought some on Sunday. But we also have Leah X. in there too," I said.

"But we have reasonable doubt," Mickey said.

"That's fine for Forsander and Samaho," I said. "But I'd like to clear it all up."

"It's not enough for me either. We have enough on Kismodel. Now we gotta nail Maydik," Leo said.

I just looked at him.

"It's a possibility," Mickey said.

"Then I'm doing okay?" Denny asked.

"You're doing fine. But there's a murderer on the loose," I said.

"Two of them," Leo said.

We kept up the speculation but didn't add anything enlightening. We finally broke up at five o'clock with everybody clearing out, including my partners. I winked at Denny as she left and hoped Mickey didn't notice.

With everyone gone I made dinner reservations. Someplace special tonight.

Then I thought about how to handle Kismodel. If anything more happened I was going to the cops with what I had. Enough of trying to handle all of this ourselves. Let the cops have some fun too. Especially Oscar Chang.

On the way over to Denny's apartment I thought I kept seeing a white Camaro behind me but when I parked on the street off Lombard it had disappeared. My imagination working overtime, I was sure.

"Where are we going?" she asked.

"A surprise."

"Am I dressed for it?"

"You bet." She looked great in a raspberry-colored sweater dress that clung to her figure like a soft second skin.

I parked in the high rise garage across from Pier 39, the shopping center created out of a working pier on the docks along the Embarcadero.

"We're eating here?" she asked. The Pier was a tourist haven; hardly where a sophisticated San Francisco P.I. would take a lady to dinner.

"I'm just parking here."

We walked by several Piers until we reached my surprise restaurant: the sailing ship Dolph Rempp.

"What a great idea!"

"It's a 1908 Danish vessel, the one they used in the original *Mutiny on the Bounty* film."

We went up the gangway and were met by a maître'd who seated us at Table 10 on the Captain's deck. We had a great view of the city and the bay. The ship rocked gently in its berth.

We had broiled Mahi Mahi for the entrée with a bottle of Gray Riesling from Napa County.

We didn't talk much during dinner. We watched the city and the harbor light up.

After cognac for dessert we left the ship and drove back to her apartment. I felt mellow and romantic but I wasn't sure what I was doing. I also forgot to check for the white Camaro.

We were sitting close together on the couch when she said, "So you are interested in some safe sex?" she said.

I was but I didn't say so.

"If you don't say anything I'll have to read your mind." She kissed me hard on the lips.

And then she came on harder. "We've all been spoiled. Look at the sexual diseases throughout history. It's only recently that we've

According to St. John

had all these wonder drugs. At no other time in history was sex safe."

She was right. And I admit I was tempted. Tell death to kiss off. We held each other.

"So you're willing to take a chance?"

The ultimate AIDS question of the eighties.

I cared for Denny. And she was beautiful and sexy. But I wasn't in love with her. I was still in love with Mickey. And finally I wasn't crazy. I could turn down Denny without feeling that my manhood was threatened.

I untangled myself from her and got up. "I'm still in love with Mickey," I said. "If we're ever together again, how would I explain all of this?"

"You mean you'd act more sexually responsible than me."

I went over by the window. "Since you put it that way, yes."

Denny put her face into her hands. "I don't know what to do. I'm scared, Jeremiah."

Trying to think of what to say, I stared out of the window. At first my eyes were unseeing. But then I couldn't miss it.

The white Camaro was parked across the street but far enough up the block that its license plate was visible. Sloppy work. It had a sun roof just like the car I had seen earlier. I wondered how to handle the situation. Direct confrontation? That would mean coming out the front door. I didn't see a way of getting behind the man in the car.

But someone coming from another direction could. I told Denny what was happening, then I called the Chief.

She pulled herself together and we buried our previous subject without remorse. I had her look out of the window.

"Does that Camaro look familiar?"

She hesitated. "I don't know. All cars look alike to me."

I wasn't satisfied with her answer but I didn't press it.

Twenty minutes later I saw the Chief walking casually along the sidewalk. It should have been the perfect surprise attack. As he approached the car I started out of the apartment. Before I could open the front door I heard a splattering of shots and the squeal of tires. I rushed out into the street to find the Chief down.

"Chief! Chief!"

He was already on his feet but there was a large circle of blood staining the pants leg of his right thigh.

"What happened?"

"The bastard in the car had a gun and he shot me and took off. That is what happened. Good thing he was such a lousy shot."

"I'll get an ambulance."

"It's only a flesh wound," he insisted.

"The bullet is in there. And you look like you're about to pass out."

"I know."

"I thought Indians moved soundlessly in their moccasins."

"I have on cowboy boots."

"Come on. I'll get you up to Denny's."

I helped him across the street and up the stairs to Denny's apartment. It was slow going since the Chief couldn't use his right leg. We laid him down on the couch.

"You have some whiskey?" I asked.

"All out. But I've got that beer you left."

"Henry's I bet. Well, it will have to do," the Chief said.

While we waited for the ambulance Denny cut up a towel and I tied a strip of it tight around the wound to stop the bleeding. While I worked the Chief drank three bottles of Henry's all the time complaining that it wasn't Budweiser. He wasn't hurt too bad if he could keep this up.

"Did you get the license?" he asked.

"Yes."

"Did you see the man?" I asked.

"He had on a black ski mask."

"Could you tell if he was white or black?" I asked.

"No. I could not even see his hands. He had on gloves."

"There goes the paraffin test. What about the gun? Did you recognize the model?"

"I was not trying to get a good look at it. It did seem foreign."

"Anything else I can do?" Denny asked as she brought over another beer.

"Yes. The next time your friend here finds someone tailing him tell him to call the police."

It turned out to be a flesh wound as the Chief had said. Accord-

According to St. John

ing to the operating physician there was minimal damage to the muscle and the Chief should recover quickly. The bullet was recovered in very good shape.

From the hospital I called Johnny D. at home and told him what happened.

"You sure this has somethin' to do with the Cole case. I know lots of people might take a shot at the Chief."

"Run this license and we'll see. It was on a white Camaro. Probably an '87 or '88."

"All right," he said, without an argument.

"And send somebody out to the shooting scene. There are all kinds of shells there. The guy was trigger happy."

"Got any other orders?"

"That'll do for now."

In ten minutes he called back. "The car is registered to Perry Maydik."

"Well?"

"I'm gettin' my ass out of bed and going to look for a judge who will issue a search warrant at this hour."

So I told him all about the Rambo attack and the tape Kismodel was after and the Llama in Maydik's filing cabinet and the director's gambling debts. "Talk to Leroy again. Kismodel was backstage as well as Maydik."

"You're withholding evidence."

"No I'm not. I just gave it to you."

"Chang is gonna be pissed."

I didn't care. I fell asleep in the chair by the Chief's bed. I slept until awakened by a standing Chief Moses supporting himself with a cane.

"What are you doing? You're supposed to stay here overnight."

"You stay if you want to. This Chief is going home to his houseboat. You can get sick in a hospital."

"What about your truck?" I asked.

"Damn! By Denny's apartment. Drive me there."

The Chief needed the cane to limp along but that was his only problem. I drove him to his pickup and asked him if he could drive it.

He got in, slammed the door, and drove away.

I accepted the visual evidence.

WILLIAM BABULA

On the way home my thoughts returned to Denny. Had she really not recognized Maydick's car? It was hard to accept considering that she did not have a perfect record with the truth so far.

23

Tuesday was election day. The hot ballot issue for me was whether the city would vote to build a downtown baseball stadium for the Giants to replace the Candlestick icebox.

I voted early at my polling place in an elementary school library, then came back to find the office open. My partners were both there.

"Did he tell you about last night?" I asked Mickey.

"All about it."

There was an edge to her voice. If she was bothered that I was alone with Denny in her apartment it was a hopeful sign. Maybe.

"How's the leg?" I asked.

"Still stronger than yours," he said.

"Want to shoot a little one-on-one?"

"Another white man taking advantage of a massacred Indian."

"Where were you, anyway?" Mickey asked. "We had to open up."

"I voted. Did you?"

They had both neglected to vote.

"Let's keep the Giants here," I said.

"Lacrosse is better," the Chief said.

"We can have both."

"Why don't we trade the Giants for the Atlanta Braves or even better the Cleveland Indians. I like their Indian logo," Mickey teased the Chief.

"And the Redskins for the Forty-Niners," he said.

The Chief had a collection of pennants hanging up in his houseboat. Under a Cleveland banner hung pennants that read: New York Jews; Washington Negroes; Kansas City Poles; L.A. Mexicans and San Francisco Yellowskins.

Everyone got the message.

"You guys have got to vote, I said. "It's going to be close."

"Maybe later," Mickey said.

The Chief started to read *The Wall Street Journal* and Mickey began typing an old report we owed to a law firm. It was about time we got to it. This was a client that paid.

I was going to go upstairs for some breakfast cereal when Johnny D. came walking into the office.

"Good news," he announced. "I got the warrant last night and we completed the searches of Kismodel's private residence and business premises. We came up with the Amanda Cole tape at his office. He looks good for subordination of assault at least. He's under arrest."

"What's he say?" I asked.

"Claimed he didn't know the tape was there. That if he knew it, he would have destroyed it."

Made sense to me, but Kismodel wasn't my problem.

"Where'd you find it?" Chief Moses asked.

"Under a stack of tapes in a cabinet."

"What about Maydik?"

"A real prize. We searched his house and his office in the theater. We came up with a recently fired Llama of the same caliber as was used on the Chief, the black gloves, and the black ski mask. And he has no alibi. He was driving his Camaro around by himself last night. We busted him for attempted murder."

Things were falling neatly into place but there was a detail nag-

According to St. John

ging at me—a piece of the puzzle that didn't quite fit—that I couldn't pin down.

"Are you going to drop charges against Denny?" I asked.

"Chang's talkin' to deputy D.A. Vorflagel right now. And I gotta get outta here."

"Join us for dinner tonight?" I asked.

"On you?" he asked.

"Sure."

"It's a deal." Then Johnny got out of there before I could come up with that troubling detail.

I called Forsander and Samaho and told Scott what was going on. He was delighted. Then I called Leo Stubbs. His wildest conspiracy dream had come true and the man was ecstatic. If it all worked out, the insurance company would be off the hook.

I left Mickey typing the report and the Chief, who had decided his leg was indeed aching like hell, lying on the couch, muttering that the pain pills weren't working. With his size he probably needed a triple dose. I took the cable car over to Denny's to give her the good news in person.

Denny was looking rested and beautiful. Her face was carefully made up and her hair had just been washed. She was wearing the kimono from that first night of bad memory. I didn't want to know if she had on anything beneath it.

We sat down on the couch. I told her about Kismodel and Maydik.

"I can't believe it," she said.

"The police have the evidence." I went on to explain.

"Then I'm in the clear."

"You bet. As soon as the D.A. agrees to drop the charges. I'm sure that's what Vorflagel will recommend. He doesn't want a loser of a case. Nobody does."

She hugged me. I felt her full breasts pressing against my chest through the silky material of the dragon robe.

This was not what I had in mind.

"I've got some work to do," I said as I suddenly got up.

"I understand."

"You saw the white Camaro last night. You must have known Maydik's car. Why did you say you didn't recognize it?"

She told me. It was my nagging detail that could create problems for us. All the same I did invite her to join us all for dinner that night. To celebrate. I hoped.

Now I did have work to do. I hit nearly every specialty car rental place and Chevy dealer in town before I came up with what I was looking for.

When I got back the Chief was asleep and Mickey was getting ready to leave.

"Where did you go?" Mickey asked.

"I needed to see Denny."

"I bet. Make up for what you missed last night? If you did miss anything."

I didn't want to get into it now. I asked, "Where are you going?"

She looked at me. "I want to change for dinner," she said.

"Don't forget to vote."

"What are you? From the League of Women Voters?"

"We've got to keep the Giants here."

"A downtown stadium in China Basin would bring a lot more traffic by my apartment. I might vote against it."

"Forget about voting," I said.

"Some voice for democracy," she said as she left.

I was going to have to answer Mickey's questions about Denny. If she still bothered to ask them. I just needed to choose the right time.

We met at Reggio's, a small Italian restaurant on Lombard, where you could wear anything from a tuxedo to a jogging suit. And people did. The menu was several pages long, the portions were large, and the prices fair.

At Mickey's request we passed on any of the veal dishes because of the conditions under which veal calves are raised. Every once in a while Mickey took to a cause.

"Any problem with how squid is treated?" I asked.

She punched my arm. She seemed in a little better mood.

I ordered the squid.

The D.A. had dropped the charges and the celebration was official.

We were drinking champagne with our food because the Chief claimed that champagne was the only thing that killed the pain in his leg.

The TV was on and the first election update gave some pretty

According to St. John

dismal numbers for the stadium. It looked like the new stadium and the Giants were dead.

"You voted against it," I said to Mickey.

"I compromised. I abstained."

"Well if they move I'll shift allegiance to the Oakland A's," I said, always ready to compromise on the burning issues.

"Good. I like their green and gold colors better," Mickey said.

"Just because they look better than orange and black on you," I said.

We toasted Denny.

The only one missing was Johnny D. but no one holds up a party for a cop.

When he finally came in, he grabbed a glass of champagne and a slice of garlic bread and sat down.

"The bullets were fired from Maydik's Llama. The ballistics match."

"That sonofabitch," the Chief groaned and rubbed his leg.

"Fast work," I said.

"Homicide gets priority. Especially when Chang is pushing."

We toasted everyone.

"Sorry we gave you a hard time, Ma'am."

"You were just doing your job," Denny said.

"Love to hear a citizen say that," Johnny said with a large grin.

We ate and drank some more and listened to another dismal election update.

Then Johnny D.'s beeper went off.

"When did you start carrying that around?" I asked.

"Chang's idea."

Johnny made his call and came back to the table.

"I got a possible homicide. Could even be a poisoning."

"Potassium cyanide?" I asked.

He shrugged. "Can't say. But it's a woman. In a room with theater posters of Amanda Cole plastered everywhere."

"Did you get a name?" I asked.

"Yeah. Rose Smith."

"Damn! That was the woman Parker Rinshell said could have been having an affair with Amanda."

"Now that's real interestin', Jeremiah," Johnny said as he started towards the door.

"Can I go with you, Johnny? Ride with a cop program?"

He hesitated. "Oh, why not? Chang's off on some other case downtown."

We beat it out of there. I knew my partners would take the tab out of petty cash.

We hadn't even started our search for Rose Smith, not even a look in the phone book, and the lady had been located for us. But in no condition to answer questions. Only to raise some new ones. A killer was still out there even though the case seemed close to a solution. How did this killer tie into Kismodel, Maydik, and what I had learned about a rented white Camaro? Denny seemed free and clear but we were still waiting for the fat lady to sing.

24

The Crime Scene Unit was crawling all over the place. Polaroid cameras whirred. The men and women in the room were collecting samples of anything that might be remotely useful. And of course they were hunting for fingerprints. The new computer technology that could conduct a print search in a few hours that would have taken a full-time employee over a year to do—with much less efficiency—has made fingerprints much more important in solving crimes. Consider the Night Stalker murders and the computer search that identified Richard Ramirez. That would have been impossible a few years ago.

The Medical Examiner was still in there with the body.

I stayed out of the way, in the hallway outside of the apartment. The place was seedy, barely a step up from a room in the Tenderloin.

Johnny D. was talking to the woman who found Rose Smith. She was a large woman with arms like hams. Her black hair was cut in a mannish style and the robe she wore revealed tattoos on her forearms and heavy cleavage.

She had come to collect the rent for November from Rose.

"You let yourself in?" Johnny asked.

"Sure. I'm the super. It's in the lease they gotta sign."

"How'd you know she'd be here.?"

"She told me she'd have the money tonight."

"She behind much?"

"She's always behind. I was ready to kick her butt out last month but she came up with two months' back rent in the middle of October."

Johnny bit his lip. He didn't seem certain about where to take it. I started asking questions of my own.

"She have a source of income?"

"Not really. And no family. But I figured she hit on some people once in a while."

"Why?"

"Like last month. She said she had a friend would give her some money. For what I don't know. But she hung on."

"Did you see any of these friends?"

"Not tonight."

"Ever?"

"No. I don't like to mess with anyone's private business. I ain't no snoop about my renters."

"You have some rough trade," I added.

"What do you mean?"

"You have hookers working out of here."

"Shit. What's he talkin' about. This is a legit apartment. But I don't snoop on private lives."

I looked at Johnny. He was content to let me continue. "Was there a name other than hers on any of the checks she paid with?"

"Only paid cash. That's how she always had her money."

I asked some more questions but that was all the useful information she had.

"Thanks for helpin' out in the interrogation," Johnny D. said to me when we were through.

"No problem." No problem recognizing his sarcasm either. "Do you have people checking the other tenants?" I asked.

"Brilliant. Now why didn't I think of that. Of course we do."

According to St. John

"Nobody in this place is going to talk."

"Rose Smith was down pretty low."

"I wonder what she did to get that money last month?"

"That's a good question, Jeremiah."

We looked into the murder room. With the CSU winding down it was less like a flea market on Sunday morning.

The room was shabby like everything else in the building. Most of the furniture wasn't even plastic or formica but compressed cardboard. It didn't need painting and cleaning; it needed fire-bombing. Even the posters on the wall, most of them from plays starring Amanda Cole, were yellow and cracking. They were held up by Scotch tape that had yellowed and cracked as well.

The M.E. was still at work, so we poked around the edges of the room. Johnny D. took out a metal strong box from the closet and pried it open. There was no money, only a few pieces of costume jewelry. And yellowed clippings. These were of reviews of Amanda Cole's performances going back some twenty years. There were even some old reviews where Rose Smith was mentioned in a bit part. These notices were easy to find. Wherever you saw something underlined in blue ink. There was one new review: Cleo Maura's review of *Macbeth*. I wondered how much Rose Smith had suffered for her love of Amanda Cole.

The M.E. was ready to talk to Johnny. I stood there and hoped he wouldn't ask who I was.

The doctor's name was Ribbs. He was one of the newer ones. Ribbs was a big man, lineman size, with a short brush cut over a pink face shaped like an anvil. He wore his clothes loose. He was wearing latex gloves. The only incongruous touch was a large pair of horn-rimmed glasses.

"Everything so far confirms my first reading of poison. We have some severe burns in the mouth and throat."

"How'd she take it?" Johnny asked.

"I'd guess in tea. There was some spilled on the floor. The lab people will analyze it. There was an unusual odor to it."

"Could it be suicide?" Johnny asked.

"No. This isn't a suicide," he said. "Somebody cleaned up. Washed the teacup with the woman dying on the floor."

"About that odor? An educated guess?" I asked.

"I'll wait for the lab report."

"What about potassium cyanide?"
"Who is this guy?" Ribbs asked.
"He's okay. There was a poisoning last month. Cocaine cut with potassium cyanide."
He nodded. "It was probably the sugar," Ribbs said. "I'm done with the body," he announced. That meant the meat wagon could haul it away.
But first Johnny and I wanted a better look at it. Rose Smith was stretched out on the floor with a look of agony on her face. The killer had been cruel.
In life Rose had been a short, dumpy, unattractive woman in her late forties. We both stared at her.
"What a way to go," Johnny said.
"Just like Amanda Cole."
"And this time Denny Belknap has all kinds of alibi witnesses," he said.
"You bet."
Johnny started to go but I stood staring at the body. There was something familiar about it but I couldn't put my finger on it.
We went out into the hall.
"She look familiar to you Johnny?" I asked.
"No. Dead people tend to look alike."
I doubted that.
We saw Detective Chang coming up the steps. He was looking around at the peeling paint with great distaste. And sniffing. There was an odor of urine I hadn't noticed before. This was not the kind of territory Chang liked.
"Shit," Johnny D. said.
But Chang just nodded at me as he passed by. Maybe he was getting mellow. Or maybe he was just tired. Or maybe he appreciated the work we had done to deliver Kismodel and Maydik. You never knew with the inscrutable Chang.
Until he stopped and smiled. Like he had just swallowed a canary and liked it.
"Constructing false evidence is a felony," he said.
"I didn't touch a thing. Ask the M.E."
"Not here, St. John. Not here."
"I don't know what you're talking about."
"Bullshit." He went into the room.

According to St. John

No more wise sayings from the man. Unfortunately I did know what he was talking about: Kismodel and Maydik, our latest homicide stars.

I had some tough decisions to make. Which meant I would have to try to put them off.

There was no way that Amanda Cole was using this dump as a love nest, but in desperation I tried the last unknown key on Amanda's ring in Rose Smith's apartment door. No way could I make it fit.

By Wednesday morning we had confirmation of the potassium cyanide. But not much else. The CSU had not come up with anything that could be tied to the killer. The fingerprint search came to zilch. It looked like I would have to resort to old P.I. technology. Kick some ass.

But first I got a call from Scott. "How about some basketball tonight? We lost another player."

"I'm not on the roster."

"So you'll be a ringer. Don't worry about it. Tony cracked a rib and he's out. You can have his shirt and number. You're about the same height and you look enough alike to fool the scorekeepers. Just don't shave your six o'clock shadow and you'll be perfect."

It was screwy but I agreed to do it. Scott and Brian needed help and I thought a little serious exercise would be good for me. I could test out the back in a full court game. And maybe expending all that physical energy would help get my stalled brain in gear.

Denny was in the clear. But I didn't believe Kismodel and Maydik had killed Amanda in a conspiracy, or that either one had acted alone. I did believe that Chang thought I framed them to get Denny off. What I needed was the real killer to clean things up.

My solution: Play some roundball disguised as somebody else. It turned out to be the smartest thing I did on the case.

That night I didn't shave again and imitated Tony's slouch and walk. I thought I did a fair job. In the locker room before the game I changed into his uniform, with the number twenty-five on the back. I brushed my hair down over my forehead like he wore it. I was ready to play the part.

"Looking good, Tony," Brian yelled at me.

Scott slapped my back. "You're exaggerating the slouch."

"Close enough," I said. "I've got so many other details right."

"Especially the uniform and the expectations of the refs and officials."

We didn't have to worry about the fans. Only a few wives and girlfriends ever bothered to show up. This was really the boys' night out.

Out on the court I had no problems except for physically trying to keep up with the pace. I was out of shape. But Tony hung in there. I was even cheered on by Tony's girlfriend from the stands with cries of "Go Tony!" We didn't fool around when it came to clever deception.

In the second half the game was still close, although our team with just five players was fading fast.

I fouled an opponent who had beaten me to the basket on a drive. Better than to let him have an easy basket. He didn't appreciate the strategic move and threatened me with a lawsuit.

"So sue me," I said for Tony.

As he moved to the foul line for his shots I heard one of the refs call to the scoring table, "Two-five," as he held up the right number of fingers to indicate my number, "With the hack—two shots."

That was Tony's third foul.

And then it came to me. Like one of the Chief's gifts from the Great Spirit. Everything had fallen into place. I had a theory that explained everything in the universe of the murder. It was perfect crime physics.

I thought of leaving the court right then to test it out. But I decided even solving a murder could wait for the end of a close basketball game. Especially one in which we could beat an all-attorney team.

"Go Deadbeats!"

The adrenaline was pumping. I got hot. My weariness was gone. The legs that had gone to rubber suddenly firmed up. We were catching up. In the eternally slow last minute I hit a jumper to tie the score.

They hit a layup with ten seconds left. We were down two. We took our final time out.

"We play for the last shot," Scott said. "Between five and three seconds so we have a chance for an offensive board if it misses.

According to St. John

Tony. You're hot. Go for a three pointer. We'll collapse if we go into overtime without any subs."

Tony was hot.

With four seconds on the clock I took a jumper from the right of the key behind a Samaho screen. I made sure I was well behind the three point line.

I expected it to be close. I expected it to spin around the rim and maybe fall through. Instead it was a perfect swisher. We were up one and they were out of time outs. A desperate half court bomb rattled the glass backboard and that was it. We won.

"Way to go Tony!" Tony's girlfriend cheered.

I passed on the keg of beer that Scott and Brian tapped after every game—win or lose. I had a key to check.

After taking care of that detail I went back to my office. I had some planning to do for tomorrow.

25

Thursday morning I was sitting up stiff and straight in my chair, waiting for my partners to arrive. It may have been Tony who got credit for twenty-one points last night but it was Jeremiah who ached in every muscle of his body. I took out a bottle of aspirin and ate two more. It was too painful to get up for water.

Finally Mickey arrived. She was polite, professional, and cool to me. A few minutes later Chief Moses came in. I called them into my office.

They both sat down on the couch, the Chief elevating his leg while he held on to his cane.

"How's the leg, Chief?" I asked.

"Slight improvement."

"Ow," I said as I shifted in my chair.

"What is wrong with you?" he asked. "You get shot in the butt?"

"A basketball game last night. With no subs."

"That's crazy. You're out of shape," Mickey said. "Now you know how I felt after all that running."

"But it's the smartest thing I've done on this case. Because I've got it."

"And I thought you practiced safe sex," the Chief said. "Just like the Great White Surgeon General Father recommends."

Mickey scowled at me. She was getting downright cold.

"No such thing," I said. "But I'm talking about the solution to the crime."

"I thought it was solved," Mickey said.

"You'll see."

"When?" Chief Moses asked.

"Patience. First we get to have some fun and keep our reputations clean with the cops."

"The man's crazy with pain," Mickey said.

"Chang thinks we framed Kismodel and Maydik to clear Denny," I explained.

"What do we do to dispel this myth?" she asked.

"We move. Is your leg up to some strain in a good cause?" I asked the Chief.

"Yes, Kimosabe," he said as he stood up. The cane looked like a formidable weapon.

I groaned as I slowly pushed myself out of the chair.

"But are you?" Mickey asked.

"I will be."

"Then let's go," she said.

Given my sore legs and the Chief's bullet wound, I sprang for a cab. It dropped us off at a building south of Market.

The three of us went directly to the L.S. Detective Agency and barged past the receptionist. She was a shrewish looking woman, with iron gray hair in a bun. She threatened to call the police.

"I don't think so," I said. I tore the phone cord out of the wall.

She screamed.

"Shut up," Mickey said.

The Chief just smiled politely.

The main office door was locked but it succumbed to two of my doorknob high kicks, a job usually left for the Chief.

Leo Stubbs was lying back in his executive chair, his mouth open, his eyes closed. He looked dead.

According to St. John

Suddenly a young woman in a very short denim skirt and a halter top out of which she was slipping jumped up from behind the desk. She had straight hair, so blond it was white, large blue eyes, and a chubby face. She was at least sixteen.

"You didn't say nothin' about a group here, Leo."

Leo returned from the dead.

"What the fuck you doin'? Whaddya do to my fuckin' door? Jesus. Are you people crazy?"

The shrewish receptionist was behind us, calling to Leo, explaining that she tried to stop us.

"Stop blubberin' and call the fuckin' cops."

"The phone's out of order," I said.

Leo reached for it anyway. The Chief covered it with his cane. And cracked Leo's fingers in the process.

"Go get the Horse!" Leo screamed to the Shrew.

The Chief laughed as she disappeared. I smiled. I had an idea who the Horse was.

"What the fuck are you doin' here?" Leo shouted at us.

"Spoiling your fun with underage girls, I hope," I said.

"I ain't finished," he told her.

"You want me to finish you now?" she asked.

"Yeah. Yeah. You heard me. You been paid already."

She looked at us. Then at Leo. "Sorry, Mister. I'm leaving."

With some remnant of grace she walked past us and out of the office.

"Sonofabitch. A shy hooker," Leo said. Then he added, "I'm really pissed off at you guys. What's the meanin' of this shit, Jerry."

"You know Leo," the Chief said.

"Detective Chang thinks I set up Kismodel and Maydik," I said.

"So?"

"You know better."

"Oh yeah. Talk to my man about it. Meet Horse Markowitz."

The Horse entered the room. Big as I remembered him.

"Rambo," I said. "Nice to see you out of uniform."

The Horse started to come at me when Mickey unleashed a swift kick to his groin. They trained her well on that Ohio police force. The Chief, slightly hampered, followed with a blow to the back of the neck with his cane. The cane splintered. Something similar happened to the Horse's neck.

"That takes care of your Horse's ass," I said to Leo. "Now it's your turn."

"What do you guys want?"

I took out a small tape recorder from my pocket. "Just for you to talk. Tell us the kinds of things you had your operative here do."

"Like what?"

"Like breaking into my office and getting the Kismodel tape. Then planting it in Kismodel's office for the cops to find. Then getting Maydik's gun and using it to shoot the Chief. And to leave a half-dozen bullets for ballistics to match up. And leaving the ski mask and gloves for the cops again. Nice work. And then of course the white Camaro. I found where you rented one the day the Chief was shot. You put me to a lot of trouble. I figure you switched the rental plates for Maydik's and then switched them back after the shooting. So his car gets made at the scene. You've been clever, I have to admit. But you know where you made your mistake? You rented a Camaro with a sunroof. Maydik doesn't have one."

That was why Denny—who wasn't very sure about the car in any case—didn't tie it to Maydik. The one thing she was sure of was that his car didn't have a sunroof. Maydik had a skin condition that forced him to stay out of the sun. As he told us, he detested the sun.

"It was the best I could do on short notice. Listen. No way the cops can prove this shit on us. We sit tight and I split the take from the insurance company with you," Leo offered.

"How much?"

"In a case like this a hundred grand if they don't pay out."

"Substantial savings," Mickey said.

"Good business," the Chief added.

"It stinks, Leo." I pulled him up by his unbuttoned shirt collar. I noticed he hadn't even bothered to zip up his fly.

"Fifty grand each," he pleaded.

I punched him in the jaw. He fell back against the chair. I pulled him back up and hit him again.

"No deal. I want you to talk to the tape. After you zip up your fly."

"Can't we come to some kinda resolution."

"We did. We won. You lost. Now talk."

According to St. John

"This kinda confession ain't gonna be worth a bucket of cold piss."

"We'll see," I said. "Besides confession is good for the soul."

"Whose?" Leo asked. Blood was dripping down the corner of his mouth.

"Mine."

The Horse stirred and Mickey sent him back out to pasture with a chop to the neck.

"I started the tape."

"You bring this to Chang and Maydik and Kismodel walk, it's your broad Belknap back in jail."

"I'll take that chance."

I started the recorder and Leo sang beautifully. He had done everything just as I had worked it out. I hoped that didn't say anything about how my mind functioned.

"They'll never get my license," he said when he was finished.

"They'll just throw you in jail."

"With Denny Belknap."

I picked up the recorder. "And Leo, the name's Jeremiah. Don't forget it."

"Don't worry, you fucker, I won't."

As we made our way over Horse's body and past the receptionist who was back at her desk acting as if nothing had happened, Mickey said, "The bastard's right. Now they'll pin it back on Denny."

"No they won't. I've got the solution."

"Are you sure?" Mickey asked.

I patted the tape. "I don't think this needs to go to Detective Chang right now. Let's make sure I'm right first."

"He is finally moving towards wisdom," the Chief said as he limped along the hallway.

"Hurt?"

"Yes."

"Me, too," I said.

Mickey just shook her head. "You old men are too much."

26

That afternoon I tried to reach our suspect by telephone. No luck.

I got out the reviews of *Macbeth* and read them over and over. I especially noted the attention paid to Lady Macbeth's appearing with the witches to tempt her husband in the opening act.

I went over my theory with my partners, daring them to shoot it down. Mickey and the Chief, as usual, did see some flaws but we worked those out. Ultimately they agreed with me. That we had not only the solution to Amanda's murder but to Rose Smith's as well. But that didn't mean we were going to the police with Leo's tape until everything was pinned down.

We decided a stakeout was necessary.

Before we took our positions Friday morning Mickey gave me a peck on the cheek and said, "Good luck, Jerry."

"Thanks, Michelle."

That got a smile out of her.

Then we got set.

I was down the street in the T-Bird and Mickey and the Chief were cruising the neighborhood in the pickup truck.

The plan was for me to go in alone. I felt I had a better chance of getting an admission of guilt if I put myself in a vulnerable position. It's a fact of the P.I. business that a suspect will brag about the crime if that suspect thinks you will be dead shortly. It's a good trick when it works. When it doesn't . . .

And I didn't want to go in with a wire. It would compromise any later criminal proceedings.

We didn't have to wait long. Our subject arrived early in the morning, apparently after spending the night out. Not atypical behavior.

I walked up the street and rang the doorbell while Mickey and the Chief parked alongside the building.

It took me ten minutes on the intercom but I finally got myself admitted.

Standing in the middle of the tiled room, sunlight pouring in from the windows of the second story gallery, the adobe tones shifting shades in lines and shadows, I went right to it and outlined my theory.

The woman, still dressed from her evening out, stared at me from the orange Aztec upholstery of the couch. She didn't offer me a Margarita or anything else.

"You were lovers and now she was leaving you," I said.

"That's crazy."

"No. That was why it had to be kept secret. Why she still used Rose Smith and even sent her money. Not the hint of a rumor about you. Both of your careers depended upon it."

"So to protect my career you say I killed her?"

"You killed her because you didn't want to lose her."

Cleo Maura leaned forward.

"This is fascinating," she said. "How was this done?"

"She never got cocaine from the Candy Man at the theater so I figure you were buying it for her. You probably gave her some at that lunch. The M.E. found metabolized cocaine in her brain. It was a way to keep her happy and in love with you. Fulfilling two needs. But it wasn't enough. So you poisoned the cocaine with potassium cyanide and watched her die."

"And where would I get this substance."

According to St. John

"Easier for you than most. It's used in photography. Just what a newspaper would have. A nice white powder to cut cocaine or sugar."

"Oh yes. Whom else was I supposed to have killed?"

"Rose Smith. Amanda's lover from a long time ago. With poisoned tea. The same poison."

She smiled. "Would you care for a Margarita?" She laughed. "But watch out for the salt."

"I'll pass."

"What about your client, Ms. Belknap, the noted actress?"

"You knew all about the fight. She was your perfect pigeon. After you killed Amanda you left some of the tainted coke on her mirror."

"This is so clever. But how did I get backstage."

"When Amanda got sick at lunch—which probably happened because she was arguing with you—you promised to deliver her some coke. So you could bring it she gave you the key to the fire door by her dressing room. That's why she couldn't get into the theater when she came by taxi. She had to be let in through the front."

"Then I must have the key. The damning evidence. Would you care to search?"

I moved towards her. "You were too clever. You replaced the key on Amanda's ring. That's the only logical explanation of why it was there. You poisoned her, then put back the key."

"Idle speculation. But I will have a drink." She got up and went to the discreet wet bar. She put some ice in a glass and poured some tequila.

"It's so clever it's a shame to tear it down. You claim I was backstage. Amanda was alive when the play began and I was in my box. Everyone could see me. I've got a theater full of witnesses. Sorry."

I was close to her now. Pressing.

"Only they weren't looking at Cleo Maura. They were looking at Rose Smith, dressed in your trademark garments. I saw the body. She was a ringer for you, Cleo."

"Sonofabitch!"

"Kind of ends your game."

"Or maybe just starts it." Cleo pulled out a mini Magnum from under the bar.

"Nice gun," I said.

"You had to be too smart ass," she said.

"How'd you get Rose to go along with the masquerade?"

"Rose was not too bright. And living close to poverty. A bad combination. Sometimes she got money from Amanda. Sometimes from me. She'd do anything no questions asked. But I told her it was all a joke. That I had to be somewhere else but I had to have everyone see me in the box opening night. Then during intermission she went into the restroom and changed. I had come in late with a regular ticket after . . . after . . . and went to the ladies' room. No one noticed me. I had the outfit in a large handbag. I changed in a stall and went up to my box after intermission. It was perfect."

"Almost."

"Almost? We'll see."

"Why'd you kill Rose."

"She kept asking for more money. To pay that damn rent. And she wanted to move to a better place. She never said so but I think she knew what I did. Or at least suspected. And she became demanding about sex. Actually coming over here. It was blackmail. I couldn't stand it any more."

"So she was a little brighter than she seemed."

"And as stupid as you."

Cleo advanced on me with the gun.

"I thought you only used poison. Guns make such a mess. Especially in such a nice house as this."

"A critic needs protection. So I have a license for a gun. I heard an intruder. Someone in the house just as I got home. I got the gun out and I shot him . . ."

"Perfect again." I tugged at my shirt. "But I'm wired."

"What?"

"I'm sending every word you say to a van outside," I lied. "Here. Feel it." I had a string tie on under my shirt. It looked like wire. I held up my hands. I wanted her in close. When she felt my shirt I let go with a right jab to the chin and then followed that with a left cross to the jaw. Nice combination. She started to drop and I grabbed her wrist and disarmed her. Then I let her fall to the tiles. I counted her out. Mike Tyson move over.

She would be out for a while. I went up to the balcony and signaled down to the street that everything was okay.

According to St. John

When I returned to the living room Cleo Maura was beginning to stir. Gradually she sat up and her eyes began to focus.

"You hit a woman."

"Only a critic."

"You bastard."

"You had the gun."

She tried to stand up but couldn't. She settled for staying on the tile floor. "What got me was how damn certain you were. How come?"

I reached into my pocket and took out Amanda's keys. I held one up. My mystery key. "It fit your gate and your door. She had to be your lover."

"I forgot to take that one off when I put back the other key. What if I had remembered?"

I waited a long time to answer. "Then it would have only been something else."

"That's what you say."

"What started me thinking was the way you didn't mention Denny playing one of the witches. Or anything before intermission. Because you didn't see half the play."

"You bastard."

It was early. Johnny D. would be just coming on to his morning shift. I wanted to give this one to Johnny, not to Chang.

"Mind if I use the phone?" I didn't wait for an answer. I called and told him to come to Cleo Maura's place.

"Whaddya got for me?" he asked.

I looked at Cleo and patted the Leo Stubbs tape I had in my pocket.

"A murderer and a dirty P.I."

27

On Saturday we could celebrate in earnest.

Horse Markowitz had turned into a talking ass and Leo would soon be history as a P.I. if not worse. The news made the Chief's leg feel much better. He didn't even bother to replace the broken cane.

Cleo Maura had been arrested and charged with two counts of murder. She was represented by one of the best defense attorneys in the city. With that going for her she might never be history.

And the Hartman Insurance Company would have to pay up on the key person policy.

"Support for Shakespeare and the arts," I announced.

Kismodel could continue with his lifestyle and pay the bill owed to Forsander and Samaho. Which was good news for us as subcontractors.

Maydik could pay off his gambling debts and start all over again. I hoped he could stay out of the casinos at Tahoe.

And the show continued to do well. Offers were coming in for new parts for Denny. She was on her way to stardom or something like it.

And Mickey, the Chief, and I were going that night to the first Warrior home game of the season. In Oakland, where the team has been playing for the past seventeen years after leaving San Francisco. That's why I worry about the Giants. So we drove to the East Bay for an early barbecue supper at a place called Earl's in Emeryville. In my opinion Earl's has the best barbecue in the Bay Area. Earl says so himself right on his sign. It was mostly a take-out joint, situated right on San Pablo Avenue, surrounded by poker parlors where gambling was legal. A vestige of the Old West.

There were a few tables in the rear by the kitchen. It was hot there but the smells made it worth it.

Earl, a black man in his fifties, always wore a green smock as an apron and a gold and green A's hat to go with his infectious grin. He was always smiling and always brandishing a slab of ribs on a giant fork. Besides ribs Earl barbecued anything that California humans ate. From pork to chicken to turkey to lamb to an occasional rattlesnake. They all came with his delicious secret sauce in mild, regular or hot.

Denny was with us. She didn't want to be left out of the real celebration. She borrowed Maydik's Camaro and was driving back for her performance that night after we ate. Even offstage she looked like an actress.

Mickey looked plain beautiful in a Warrior sweatshirt, warm up jacket, and jeans.

After we ordered I went over my now proven theory.

"Amanda was upset at lunch because Cleo threatened to reveal their relationship," I said.

"But that would destroy Cleo as an objective critic," Denny said. "I don't see how she could have kept her job."

"Cleo didn't care. She didn't need the money. She was going to take them both down in flames. I imagine she threatened to reveal Amanda's coke habit as well."

"Which of course she fed," Mickey noted.

"These white women are unnatural. We had ways of dealing with such women in our tribe."

According to St. John

"I don't want to hear," Denny and Mickey said together.

The Chief kept quiet.

I cleared my throat for attention. "But Amanda wouldn't stay with Cleo no matter what the consequences. Cleo didn't want to lose her so she took the other extreme lover's position. She would kill her. I'm not sure when the plot formed in her mind but she had two nice patsies to set up. Rose Smith and Denny Belknap."

"According to you, Jeremiah, this all came together for you during a City League basketball game?" Mickey asked.

"According to St. John, that's how it happened. Brilliant, huh?"

"The sun is brilliant," the Chief snapped.

I spelled it out anyway. "I was a ringer brought in for an injured player. No one noticed the switch. I was Tony. I had his number and his uniform and I looked enough like him. Which made me think of Halloween, my visit from Rambo, women with men's names, actors in drag, even Denny dressed as Cleopatra, and finally a ringer for this Cleo. A lot of things pointed to her for me but she seemed to have a perfect alibi, so I always wrote her off. Then I saw Rose Smith. Perfect for the part of Cleo. A ringer like me. Only now dead."

"And you were so sure it was Cleo Maura?" Denny asked.

"I tried Amanda's key at Cleo's place before I did anything. Just in case. When it fit I knew I was right."

The barbecue came. We tore into pork rib slabs, lamb slabs, beef slabs and some sliced beef and turkey. Hold the snake today. The baked beans were as good as baked beans can be.

This was no place to be fancy. We all had a dozen napkins and shared two pitchers of the light beer that Earl had on tap. No one complained.

Denny finished first and said as she patted her lips with a napkin, "I've got to get back for the performance tonight."

We all cleaned ourselves up with the pile of napkins and embraced her one by one.

"What's next for you?" I asked.

"We're going to tour with *Macbeth* and then I'm going to play a white Juliet to Maydik's Romeo."

I wondered how that would fly. Maydik was a little old for the teenage look. I asked, "Will there be a nude scene?"

"God. Is that all you think about?" Mickey said.

"These days," I noted.

The Chief just shook his head.

"Actually there will be one. It's Perry's trademark as a director. When Romeo and Juliet consummate their marriage. The poetry is beautiful and we're going to test the limits of stage nudity."

I didn't know there were any. I said, "Good luck, Denny."

I gave her one last kiss. A lingering one on the lips. And as I kissed her I kept wondering about her and Maydik. Had Amanda Cole been right? A mystery I didn't care to solve. We broke off the kiss.

Mickey was watching us.

"Goodbye," I said. And I meant it.

She left Earl's to drive off into the west towards the Oakland Bay Bridge.

"Hope you enjoyed that," Mickey said to me.

"I did."

Her throat flushed but she didn't say anything more. We finished eating and drinking.

After a recovery period we drove south to the Coliseum Arena for the Warrior game.

My partners complained even more than usual about the T-Bird. Of course they were stuffed, which made it difficult for them to get comfortable.

I assured Mickey that with the money from this case we would get computers for the office. But she had to shut up about the car.

"For how long?" she asked.

"Until we get home tonight." I didn't want to destroy the tradition completely.

"And you must get an alarm system," the Chief said. "I don't want to come in some Monday morning and find you dead on the floor."

"I appreciate your concern."

"There is also the matter of dead body odor. Hard to take in the morning."

"We go for the alarm system too."

The seats for the game were decent—unlike the Warrior performance.

According to St. John

"They could use a few ringers from the Lakers," Mickey suggested.

"Like five," the Chief concluded.

On the court below us ten black giants were floating as gracefully as ballet dancers through the arena air.

Unfortunately, only those in the dark visiting uniforms were doing any scoring.

It was going to be a long season.

28

After the game we stopped for some more beer at the Chief's houseboat on Mission Creek. From the outside the structure looked like a badly weathered redwood pyramid with the top sliced off. The Chief said that it was the only one he could afford. He made up for the exterior on the inside. The houseboat was the Chief's den, bachelor pad, and bedroom all rolled into one. He had soft black leather furniture, sunken lighting, and a Chief size water bed. On the walls were erotic Oriental etchings, his mock-racist pennants, and a lifesize poster of Chief Moses himself in an FSU football uniform.

Underfoot was a white rug that you had to take your shoes off to walk on. And there was a black metal freestanding fireplace. The whole thing rocked gently with the tide.

The Chief did not have Henry's or wine. Just his beloved Budweiser in cans. It was because he loved to crush the cans with two fingers. But why Bud?

"Minorities are product loyal," he explained for maybe the hundreth time since I've known him.

So we drank Bud. They didn't complain about my car, and I didn't complain about his beer.

We got talked out and tired quickly.

I drove Mickey home to her apartment. We got out of the car together and walked to the entrance doors. I held one open for her and we entered the lobby. She hit the elevator button. Given how cool Mickey had been acting towards me, I wasn't expecting anything. I had nothing planned.

"Are you going to see Denny tonight?" Mickey asked.

"No," I said. "Why?"

"Your other evening was cut short when the Chief was shot."

"You mentioned that already."

"I saw how you kissed."

"That was goodbye."

"Why?"

"She's theater people."

"What does that mean?"

"A lot of things." I took Mickey's hand. "But mainly that I care for you."

She shook her head.

"It won't be like before. I won't ask for a commitment."

She stepped into the elevator. The door stayed open.

"I'll have to think about it."

An improvement in our relationship. But I still asked, "Why?"

"Because of you and Denny. You're going to have to be honest with me."

"What do you mean?"

"Normally I would say none of that was my business. But Denny told me about her ex-husband's bisexuality. And the rest of it."

Silence.

"I didn't sleep with her."

"You had motive, means, and opportunity. I'm sure about the means."

I laughed. "How can I prove my innocence." It didn't seem like the right word but I went with it.

"Remember Vincent and his boyfriend? You can't."

"You came close on that one. It was as good as you could do."

According to St. John

"Can you do better?"

"Will you give me a chance to try?"

She nodded. The elevator door closed. I didn't try to stop it. Not tonight.

I walked past my car and then down to the waterfront. I could still see Mickey's apartment building. Clouds had covered the stars and obscured the moon.

I listened to the hard slapping of the waves against the piles. A stiff breeze came off the bay and it was cold.

I shivered.

Then I heard raindrops on the water and on the dock. They started to fall on me. I was standing in the first rain of autumn.

And I was alone.

I walked back to the car. I looked at Mickey's lights and reconsidered. I thought of going up.

I shivered again.

And then her lights went out.

I stood there, looking at darkened windows, getting soaked by a cold November rain.

There was no where else I wanted to be.